A Nest of Rats

A NEST OF RATS

John Wainwright

ST. MARTIN'S
NEW YORK

Droll rat, they would shoot you if they knew
Your cosmopolitan sympathies
(And God knows what antipathies).

Break of Day in the Trenches
                    ISAAC ROSENBERG

PART ONE

THE CATCH

Some interesting sport may be had by catching a good supply of rats in traps with the aid of ferrets, and afterwards coursing them in a good open field.

RAT

The Harmsworth Encyclopaedia

ONE...

There she is. Twisted, boneless and stupid; with her skirt ruffled up above her thighs, and with one leg of her stocking-tights badly torn at the knee; with one mule missing, and the other hanging to its foot by the toe; with her eyes wide, and her mouth still fighting for a last breath she couldn't suck in.

There she is – twisted, boneless and stupid ... and very dead.

TWO...

There was a problem. Not an insurmountable problem; not insurmountable because, if you have influence in certain quarters, and if men who operate in such quarters owe you a debt of gratitude, no problem is insurmountable. Any-thing – *everything* – can be fixed. There is an answer ... all it needs is finding.

I bathed, ran the electric razor over my cheeks and chin, then dressed with my usual care before I left the house.

I took the Volvo and drove north. I drove carefully; not pushing the needle past the thirty mark, not jumping the traffic lights, giving all the right signals and keeping in the correct lanes. To have had a shunt – to have been flagged down by some over-enthusiastic flatfoot – would have been the sad end of a beautiful freedom.

I reached Rawle's place without mishap.

There are some nice places in the Regent's Park area. Parts of that area should be called 'Millionaire's Gulch', because the monthly running cost of some of the flats and maisonettes would damn near keep the starving hordes of India off the streets for a whole year.

Rawle's pad was one such place.

The ape with the iron muscles – the one Rawle laughingly called his 'manservant' – answered the door, then shambled ahead of me, up the stairs and into the gymnasium.

It was (architecturally speaking) the fourth guest bedroom, converted. It had bars, ropes, balls and bags. It had rowing-machines, cycling-machines, massage-machines and weight-lifting-machines. It didn't have a ring ... but that's about all it *didn't* have.

It was Rawle's pride and joy. He spent half his waking life in that room, working off the fat. The other half, he spent shoving expensive food and drink into his face, to put the fat there in the first place ... but, when you own what Rawle owned, that type of cockeyed luxury isn't a luxury any more.

Rawle was spread-eagled under a multiple bank of ultra-violet and infra-red lamps. Except for eye-cover, he was mother-naked; on his back and (would you believe?) on a carpet of pure nylon 'grass'.

He was a very unpretty sight.

As I entered, he rolled his head, pointed the goggles protecting his eyes in my direction, and grunted, 'Yeah?'

The way he said it. The manner in which he asked that simple question. Tell a man, half-way through a ten stretch, that tomorrow is Tuesday ... his reply will carry the same keen interest Rawle's 'Yeah?' carried.

I waited until the ape had ambled beyond the closed door of the gymnasium.

I squatted on a bench, beyond the glare of the lamps, then said, 'Rawle, I've never asked a favour before.'

'But, now you're gonna break the habit ... right?'

I nodded. I couldn't see the eyes, behind those dark lenses, but I knew what they'd be doing. Watching. Watching *my* eyes; probing for the first flicker which might – which just *might* – be the give-away to some double-cross. Rawle trusted nobody – except, maybe, Rawle ... and, even *him* not too far.

I played for a little time.

This was necessary. I knew Rawle. Not well – no man could claim to know Rawle well – but as well as most men, and well enough to know that a big, fat, negative zero was already building up inside his brain. All his life Rawle had given nothing for nothing; if he could have put a price tag on the air he exhaled, he'd have either bottled it, or figured out some trick of holding his breath forever. That was Rawle ... and he was waiting for the space into which he could slip the word 'No'.

We did a one-way staring act for a few moments; I stared at twin discs of dark glass, and knew eyes were staring back at me from their hiding-place.

I said, 'We have some nice things going for us, Rawle.'

'I have some nice things going for me.' He carefully corrected the pronouns, and I made believe not to notice.

'Together,' I said. 'You handle vice and protection. I take care of the gambling ... and, luckily for me, a lot of people gamble.'

'Yeah. A lot of men shag and scream ... so, what next?'

'Just – y'know ...' I moved my shoulders. 'Things are cosy.'

The sweat ran in rivulets, down his artificially tanned gut. It gathered, in a globule, at his navel, then spilled over and oozed its way down his side, to soak into the green nylon.

'Things ain't as cosy as they were,' he grunted.

'No?'

'Not as cosy as they were before *you* arrived.'

I frowned pretended puzzlement, and said, 'How come?'

'You're here begging for favours.'

'Yeah. A small thing, but ...'

'So-o ... things ain't as cosy.'

'I've not yet asked,' I protested.

'So?'

'Already, you're beefing.'

'It ain't small,' he growled.

'Until I tell you what it is ...'

'It's big. It's a big, big favour. I know it.'

'It's important,' I admitted. 'But that doesn't mean ...'

'It sticks in your craw. You can't even *say* it. That's how big it is.'

He rolled until his back was to me, and jabbed at a button-switch on the wall. The bank of lamps dimmed to nothing, the canopy raised itself, then tilted and tucked itself neatly into an alcove. The gimmickry ended when shutters slid from left and right, closed the alcove and hid the lamps.

It seemed that Rawle had had his day's quota of plastic sunshine.

He grunted and wheezed himself to his feet. He ran his hands down his sides and down his outer thighs, collecting sweat on the way. He flicked his fingers, and the sweat made dark marks on the polished floor of the gymnasium.

Rawle was a great one for gestures, and I knew he was telling me things. He was telling me my worth, and what he could do to me, if he so minded ... and with what ease.

As he lifted the goggles to his sweat-soaked forehead, he said, 'Now the shit comes off. Stick around.'

As he padded from the gymnasium his feet left prints, like pug-marks of a prowling big cat, out for its evening prey.

Me? I was left with a room full of muscle-building machinery, which I didn't want, and a brain full of lousy memories, which I could have done without.

THREE...

Consider...

For twenty years, you have been married. Happily married ... or so *you* believed. You have given your wife all the respect any woman could wish for. No two-timing. No strange beds, or temporary bed-swerving. No secrets. One woman – 'for better or for worse' ... which, with her eyes wide open, is what she opted for.

On the debit side, she married a crook and, for seven of those twenty years, she has lived alone ... albeit, in comparative luxury. For seven of those twenty years you, too, have lived alone. Alone, in a cell shared by two nauseant, unwashed oafs. Alone in a place of keys and bars – of steel-shod landings and ever-locked doors – of stinking slops and granite walls.

Those seven years learned you your lesson. Not the locks, or the bars – not the stench, or the stupid regimentation – these things you could have tolerated, one day at a time ... which is the only way in which a prison sentence *can* be tolerated.

Not these things, but the separation. The separation was the *real* punishment. The separation, plus the visits, which only emphasised, and reminded you of, the separation.

Men serving prison sentences swear they will go straight. They swear an oath on it ... and, at the time, they mean it.

I, too, swore that oath, and I *did* mean it.

I was sent down, because I was one of the top half-dozen vault-men in the United Kingdom – maybe in the whole world – and, because I was good, I became careless.

The men who reached for my collar were not careless, but I bear them no grudge. They were only fractionally less

13

clever than I but, unlike me, they took no chances. I dodged them for ten days – long enough to make sure the loot would work to keep Muriel well clear of the breadline – then, I allowed myself to be caught, pleaded 'Guilty' and left all the other arguments to the insurance people.

She waited – we both waited – and, after an eternity, the seven year wait ended.

No questions were asked. No confession was volunteered ... or even expected. Seven years is a long time in which to sleep alone, and certain thoughts – certain mental images – were merely part of my punishment. They always are. Every man who loves a woman suffers this *extra* punishment, whenever he is convicted and imprisoned. A subtle punishment, rarely mentioned. A punishment which embitters, and which no amount of television, film shows, books or visits can ever allay.

Because, he never really *knows*.

If he has sense, he doesn't *want* to know. He doesn't ask. When the prison door opens, to allow him freedom he, himself, closes a door. A mental door; a door which (again, if he has sense) he locks, and seals, and never re-opens.

For six years, I played the game according to those strict rules.

I quit the vault game. I used what was left of the money to lease a glorified cesspit in the Hammersmith area. I was crazy ... that's what people said, behind my back. Hammersmith was too far beyond the orbit of clubland; a casino – even a straight casino – hadn't a hope in hell at *Hammersmith*.

People can be very wrong.

I took legal advice. That casino stayed well within the law; there was no back-room, side-room or any other damn room the cops shouldn't know about. It was legit gambling, all the way ... and, if it wasn't legit, it wasn't there.

Within a year, I'd opened another place. This time, at Fulham. Then another – then another ... six years saw

Martin Casinos at Hammersmith, Fulham, Battersea, Kensington, Willesden and Hendon. I let the smart boys do their own thing, around the Dean Street district. I didn't trespass. Unlike them, I gave my suckers an even break ... so *my* suckers came back.

I even accepted Rawle, without any bitching.

Why not?

Anybody who hits pay-dirt in the Smoke either pays, or goes under ... that's the law, beyond the law. Like bedbugs crawling beneath every comfortable blanket, the terror boys demand their quota of blood; that, or they make damn sure the bed can never be slept in.

Rawle was big in this field. He headed no recognised 'firm'. He confined himself to no carefully marked-out 'territory'. He was unique, in that he was a rogue animal who roamed, freely. He picked, and was big enough to choose his own pickings.

The organised mobs hated him. The top three, or four, could have tamed him, but the gutters would have carried blood – Rawle would have seen to that – and, in destroying Rawle, they'd have destroyed themselves ... and Rawle would have seen to *that*, too.

I was 'approached'; without actually twisting it, my arm was given a memory-jogging squeeze, and I was wise enough to receive the message. Indeed, I was wise enough to do more than receive the message ... I was wise enough to choose my own 'protector'.

I chose Rawle.

More than that, I made him the proverbial offer he couldn't refuse – a percentage of the Martin Casino takings ... whilever the Martin Casinos remained operative and undamaged.

It was a good choice ... as I knew it would be. The original 'or else' crowd aired their mouths, in protest. But, only once. A squad of Rawle's iron men demolished two joints on *their* payroll and, after that, everybody knew where everybody else stood.

That was me, then. Andrew Martin. Law-abiding owner of a chain of legit casinos, with Rawle a sleeping partner nobody wished to awaken. Happily married, to a wife called Muriel. Father of a nice, teenage kid called Anne. Living in a comfortable home, at Putney ... without a worry in the world.

Until a couple of hours before.

A couple of hours before, I'd had my balls kicked clear of their hanging-basket. But good! ... and, for no reason at all.

All that crap about 'something bigger than both of us'. But *I* was excluded from the 'us' part. Tears? Sure, there'd been tears ... there isn't a dame in the world who doesn't think she can wipe the blackboard clean of chalk, with tears. Some fink called Albert – how's that for a fink's name? ... and I didn't even *know* him. He was waiting for her – I got the whole progress report ... he was *waiting* for her. At Kennedy Airport, from which point they would 'start a new life'.

She even showed me the ticket – the passport – the entry visa – the whole shooting match ... just to make sure I got the picture into perfect focus.

Roses round the door – happy ever after – and screw the years *you've* worked your guts out for me, Andrew ... *darling*.

Rawle returned to the gymnasium. His hair was damp from the shower, and he was wearing a towelling dressing-gown, cork-soled bathroom slippers and a cigar of which Churchill himself would have been proud.

He lowered his bulk onto the platform of the weight-lifting-machine, stared across at me, and waited.

'It's a favour, Rawle,' I said, and my voice had a dry, harsh quality.

'Yeah ... you said.' He spoke with his lips – with his teeth clamped onto the thick cylinder of tobacco leaf – and the words came out accompanied by irregular puffs of cigar smoke.

'I'll pay,' I rasped.

'How much?'

'Your price. Just name it.'

'That makes it big.' His eyes narrowed, and spilled suspicion. 'An open cheque. That makes it very big.'

I moistened my lips, steadied my voice, then said, 'I want a body shifting.'

He grinned around the cigar, and said, 'I ain't no undertaker, Martin.'

'You know what I mean,' I said, flatly.

'No. Tell me.'

I told him.

The voice which told the story seemed to come from a distance; from another part of the gymnasium. It didn't even *sound* like my voice. Come to that, it didn't sound like *anybody's* voice. It was without rhythm, without rise and fall, without varying speeds. It was like the noise of electronic wizardry, when the bright boys gear a computer to recite some nursery rhyme.

The noise told the story, and Rawle listened and, when the story ended, Rawle removed the cigar from his mouth, tilted his head and blew grey-blue smoke at the ceiling.

'Well?' I asked.

Rawle rolled the cigar between his fingers, returned it to his teeth, then said, 'You have a problem, Martin.'

'You can do it,' I insisted.

'Sure,' he agreed.

'*Will* you do it?'

'Who knows?'

'Name your price.' My voice was little more than a whisper.

'We-ell, now.' His teeth grinned, around the cigar. 'I

17

could ask for the whole Martin Casino set-up.'

'The hell you could!' I gasped.

'Hey, sweetie-boy.' The grin lost itself. 'All I do is pick up a phone ... okay? All I do is give a coupla names and an address ... okay? You're in slam for twenty, and I *get* the Martin Casino set-up ... and for the cost of a phone call. You with me?'

'You wouldn't,' I breathed.

The return of the grin answered me ... the hell he wouldn't!

It is known as 'being over a barrel'. Christ! I was over a whole hogshead.

The play was his. Every stroke. Every pitch, every toss, every throw-in, every no-ball. I was crazy. I was dumb. But, I was neither crazy enough, nor dumb enough, to waste energy or emotion on argument. Rawle had me by the short hairs and, if he fancied a flying-trapeze act while he was holding them, that was *his* prerogative.

I stonewalled my expression, and waited.

Rawle tried to outwait me but, this time, the ball was in my court. Why not? He carried the trump card, and he'd shown it ... so, what else? He either played it, or he didn't play it. My only half-sane tactic was to wait for him to decide.

The waiting – the eyeball-to-eyeball silence – goosed him a little. He frowned and, gradually, the frown grew up into a scowl.

'It don't mean much ... eh?' he grunted.

I didn't answer.

'I asked you a question, Martin,' he snarled.

In a voice, as stonewalled as my face, I said, 'I didn't catch it.'

'You don't give a damn? Granite don't mean a thing?'

'I give a damn,' I countered.

'Sweetie-boy, you'd *better*.'

'But what the hell can I do about it?'

18

It was move and counter-move and, gradually, I realised a truth. Without meaning to – without even trying – I'd dimmed some of Rawle's glow. How the hell? ... I couldn't even guess. He still had me over the same, man-sized barrel. He could still flip me into a police cell, with as little effort as it would take to lift a telephone receiver ... *but, he wasn't going to do it.*

Don't misunderstand me. I was no poker player; I hadn't called his bluff. I knew Rawle and, whenever the boom started to swing, Rawle scared the very crap out of me. Calling Rawle's bluff would have been a little like calling the bluff of a tiger, half-way through its spring.

We performed more waiting and more watching.

What else? ... with me, what the hell else was left?

Then, Rawle's eyes lowered, he removed the cigar from his teeth and he spoke to the half-inch or so of grey-white ash. He spoke softly. Musingly. As if voicing his thoughts, and quietly exploring the merits, and demerits, of as yet unexplored possibilities.

He said, 'Nobody likes prison, Martin.'

'Nobody,' I agreed ... and I matched him, voice-for-voice, in gentle non-emotion.

After a pause, he said, 'What you're asking, ain't difficult.'

'What *you're* asking is a very high price,' I countered.

He said, 'It ain't difficult ... but it's damn dangerous.'

'Not with your organisation.'

'You'd have me, sweetie-boy.' He nodded his head, once, at the ash of the cigar. 'Right there ... where the fire is.'

'Yeah ... but, you'd have me, too.'

'I already have.'

It was a statement of fact. It didn't require an answer.

He said, 'So-o ... what do I do, Martin?'

'A little mutual trust?' I suggested.

His lips bowed into a slow smile, as he murmured, 'Okay

... now sell me the idea of fairies in the window-box.'

I leaned forward a fraction of an inch, and said, 'I've never welched, Rawle. Why should I double-cross?'

'Why should anybody?' he sighed. 'But they *do*.'

'I ask a favour,' I said, gently.

'Yeah ... everybody asks favours.'

'Not a big favour.'

'Not impossible,' he agreed, mildly.

'And you build a wall.'

'I discuss things, sweetie-boy. That's all ... discussion.'

'Some discussion!'

'Ain't everybody doing it, these days?'

'You wave a price tag.'

'Nothing for nothing, sweetie-boy.'

'One hell of a price tag.'

'Too much?' he asked.

'Way out.'

'Okay.' He frowned, sadly, at the cigar ash. 'What chips had you in mind?'

'A bigger percentage?' I suggested, tentatively.

'Uhuh.' He shook his head, slowly.

'Okay,' I said. 'Come down from Everest.'

'Favour for favour,' he murmured.

'Yeah ... within reason.'

He raised his eyes, looked at my face, then said, 'I need a bust.'

'No way.' I shied away from the suggestion.

'Favour for favour,' he repeated, softly.

'I'm straight, Rawle. These days, I'm straight.'

'You *were*.' The slow smile crept across his mouth, again. 'That ain't gonna be a red hot answer to a murder charge ... would you say?'

And that was it. Nothing for nothing ... or, as Rawle saw things, favour for favour. He could have found some other guy; maybe not as good – they don't take pains to learn their trade, these days – but good enough. It would

have cost him; Rawle's pie was baked with pure muscle ...
anybody with either skill or brains was missing. So, why the
hell should he pay, when he had *me* on the end of a
wire?

It made sense. Even to me, it made sense.

So-o, we argued a little. I wriggled around a little. But
the hook was fast, and the line was tight, and he had me ...
and, that was definitely *it*.

'Okay. Where, and when?' I asked, heavily.

'I'll let you know.'

'I need planning time, Rawle. These things are only easy
if ...'

'Martin,' he warned. 'You do it ... okay? You do it *your*
way. What you ask for, you get. Men, equipment ... everything. But I say when. And, till I'm ready, nobody knows
where.'

The body was dumped. They even cleaned up the mess ...
but don't ask me who the hell 'they' were.

I left a key with Rawle then, on his advice, I took a taxi to
the West End and was over-charged to watch an over-long
film which took around three hours to say sod-all. A
gangster movie, with some smooth-faced runt doing a tenth-
rate Bogart routine; all guns under the armpit and lines
delivered out of the corner of the mouth. Jesus! The creep
who wasted those few miles of celluloid had never met the
real gorillas; the bastards who *don't* have candy-floss hearts;
the bastards who don't have *hearts* ... period.

After the show, I walked to the Strand Corner House, sat
in The Trident for more than an hour, and shoved good
seafood down my gullet.

Hell knows what it was ... I left the choice to the waiter,
and didn't taste a thing.

Then, a taxi to pick up the key, the Volvo back to Putney
... and no more Muriel.

She didn't exist.

She'd never even been around. She hadn't even been born ... and some fink was likely to wait the rest of his life, at Kennedy Airport.

Judas Christ!

I got stinking drunk ... what else?

FOUR...

Kids!

Just who the hell do they think they are? Just *who*? They act like the rest of history has all been for their personal benefit; that they're the first generation to shin down the banana tree, and walk upright.

And – dammit to hell – we let 'em.

Anne gave me a white-hot roasting, when she arrived home from the flash finishing school, somewhere on the lower slopes of the French Alps. I'd sent for her. I had my story, neat and pat. The truth – as it *should* have been ... that was my line. I was the heartbroken hubby. The loving papa, seeking sweet consolation from his adoring daughter.

My aching back!

I never knew eighteen-year-olds even *knew* that language. Some finishing school ... I'd have saved myself a small fortune, by apprenticing her to the nearest bargee.

'What the hell!' I bawled. 'She's been two-timing me for years. Do you have some crazy idea that I'm going to send a search party out for her?'

'She's known Albert for less than a year,' she snapped.

'Albert *who*? I don't even know the tom cat's second name.' I held up my hand, as she opened her mouth, and yelled, 'No! Don't tell me ... I'm not interested enough to *want* to know. And, anyway,' I added, 'how the hell come *you* know?'

'We confided.'

'You – you...' I damn near choked.

'She had to confide in *somebody*.'

'Great. Why the hell not *me*?'

'Assuming she had. What would you have done?'

'Strangled the bastard,' I snarled.

'And mother? What would you have done to her?'

That was a question I didn't care to answer.

She answered it for me.

She snapped, 'You'd have made life hell for her. As a husband, you've been as much good as a quick fart on a toilet seat...'

'Where the hell d'you...'

'...and, if she'd *told* you, you'd have been a bloody sight worse.'

'Hold it!' I shouted. 'Hold it, right there.'

'Why?' she sneered. 'Is what I'm saying hitting you in the balls?'

'What you are saying,' I choked, 'is not meaning too much. But the *way* you're saying it ... Christ, you might at least wrap it up in French.'

'I can do that, too, if it's...'

'I don't want to hear it,' I bawled. 'English, French, German ... who the hell cares? *I* could have taught you sewer-talk. I was brought up on it. I know it all ... even words *you* don't know. But I wanted better things ... okay? I wanted the language clean, however hell dirty the mind was.' I cooled off a little, and pleaded, 'Anne, honey, I'm up the wall. Okay, your ma confided in *you* ... that hurts my pride, a little, but it's unimportant. That she had things to *confide* ... that's what knocks me out. She had no *reason*. I'm a one-woman man ... she knew that.' I hurriedly corrected myself. 'She *knows* that. She's *always* known that.'

'Well, grab that!' she mocked. 'One-woman man?'

'It's the truth.'

'So, what?'

23

'It means something.' I was upping the decibel rate, again.

'Not much. Not always.'

'What the hell do you know about...'

'You bored the tits off her,' she spat. '*That's* the truth. She married a man with fire in his belly ... and ended up with a husband whose guts are full of slop.'

'She – she told you *that*?' I gasped.

'Scores of times.'

'I – I don't...' I took a deep breath, then exploded, 'The damn casinos. What the creeping hell! I worked myself stupid keeping straight. I walked a bloody tightrope, so she'd never...'

'She wanted you to fall on your arse, occasionally.'

'I went bloody straight, for her sake. Even the cops knew I'd...'

'Screw the cops!'

'You don't know what you're...'

'She wanted you, as you *were*. That's all. She didn't want the creep you've *become*. Christ, it was like landing Burton ... then finding yourself with Donald Duck.' Some of the heat left her. She shook her head, in despair, sighed, then said, 'Shit. You'll never understand. Not these days. A glorified Bingo caller. How the hell *can* you understand?'

She flounced out of the room leaving me to what thoughts I could grab before my whole braincase took off for inter-stellar orbit.

Can *you* figure it out? Can *you* see the skewball sense – the tinpot logic – that makes a woman want a crook for a husband? A good woman, too. Not from a bent family ... nothing like that. A woman who worried, if she gave wrong change. Who paid every bill, right on the nail, and took credit from nobody. *That* sort of woman.

Her mother had died – killed in a rail crash – before she'd reached her second year and, from then on, her father

24

had brought her up well. He'd been a man-and-a-half; a dock-worker, and built like a bull. A union man, who'd starved in the cause of Socialism. A bastard, or a saint, depending upon which side of the fence you happen to have been, but a religious man – a chapel man – who'd opposed our marriage every inch of the way.

While I was inside, he'd visited me ... once. He'd threatened to kill me, if I ever *looked* at his daughter after I'd done my stretch.

He'd meant it, too, but they'd buried him – burned out and knackered in the cause of his beloved Socialism – two years before the end of my own seven piece.

So, what do you do for the daughter of a man like that?

You go straight ... what the hell else?

You blow the whistle on all the can-opening caper. You look around. You find something legal – something solid and respectable – something that keeps the home fires well stoked, but without the wig-and-ermine spin-off.

You come up with casinos. Legit, straight-down-the-line casinos.

And, for that, my own daughter sized me up as a creep. Sweet Jesus!

Okay, I used solicitors and I used accountants. Why not? ... I was in business. My business was gambling. Like football pools. Like stocks and shares. Like putting money into some show. Like merchant-bank chess play. No different ... except that my business was *called* gambling.

I was no less a business-man.

Which meant ... ?

Okay, it meant an image. And the image went with pin-striped trousers and brief-cases ... and pin-striped trousers and brief-cases went with unimaginative creeps.

She was wrong – sure she was wrong ... a kid her age couldn't understand these things. But that was her line of thought. Stupid. Back-to-front. All creeps had brief-cases,

25

therefore all brief-cases had creeps attached ... *that* brand of mental arithmetic.

We-ell, brother, once or twice, over the years, I'd bent a little in the breeze. I hadn't snapped; always Muriel, and what I owed Muriel, had countered the sway. But now, Muriel wasn't around. Just Anne – a daughter who bawled me out, because I wasn't an exciting enough daddy ... so, *okay*. I still had the hands, I still had the know-how, and I could still open the door on an old-fashioned Chubb while lesser men fumbled around with sardine cans. Up there, above the eye-line, all the knacks were in their various drawers. All the ingenuity. All the once-upon-a-time flair.

So, watch my tail, little daughter. Watch for the sparks, honey.

One day – some day – you are likely to have that skirt of yours blown off by the draught.

They were stupid thoughts, but they stayed with me. They grew. They became magnified. Eventually, they became nostalgia ... which is memory, with the bad bits filleted out.

Anne, for all her fire and spit, must have felt *something*. Why not? I was her father, wasn't I? She'd originated in my loins ... the only kid I'd ever sired. She had to feel *something*. She wrote goodbye notes to her buddies, at the finishing school, and moved into the Putney house, to stay. She'd come home – she left no doubt about that – and, at first the prospect scared me a little.

I sighed ... but, deep down, I wasn't sorry.

It meant taking care. It meant watching my tenses, and living a hundred-per-cent, twenty-four-hour, day-in-day-out lie. It became a habit; a deliberate, self-imposed habit of thought. And it worked. Within a week, I found myself half-believing what I knew damn well was a lie. For hours – sometimes whole days – my own mind accepted what I worked to make the rest of the world accept; that Muriel was out there, in cowboy-land, spring-interioring it with some fink called Albert.

I swear . . . I came to *believe* it.

Meanwhile, and with equal care, I gradually changed my life-style.

FIVE...

It took me three days to find Len; two days to decide I needed him, then three more days to trace him. Five days, in all.

I went round all the casinos; checked that things were ticking over, smoothly; hinted, to each manager, that I was testing semi-retirement for size – that, if I liked the feel, they'd each be onto a percentage of the takings, as a bonus for the extra responsibility – then dumped the brief-case, and started looking for Len.

I thought it was going to be easy. Find the right wire, follow the transistors and, at the other end, Len would be waiting for me. That's what *I* thought.

Friend, I picked up more old threads – including some I'd damn near forgotten – and they all welcomed me back into the fold. Time was, I'd been among the élite and, already, legends had been built around my name. Martin – who, given the time and a bent hairpin, could figure his way into Fort Knox . . . that sort of thing.

I was human. I liked it . . . and I liked and respected the guys who welcomed the return of the prodigal son.

Crooks – like cops, like all other men on God's earth – come in varying shades. The black bastards; the tearaways; the apes; the frighteners . . . who the hell likes *them*? Whichever side of the law they're on, whatever their profession, however they earn their bread, they are animals. They have no humour. No compassion. No pride. They don't

27

deserve the right to walk upright ... none of 'em!

But the others. The second-storey boys. The con men. The various experts in their own particular line ... they're nice people. They inhabit their own world, and their world is as decent, and as moral, as the other world. They marry, and have kids, and they are good husbands and loving fathers. Their *work* is a little off-beat ... that's all.

Their tastes are like yours. Their hurts and their indignations. Everything about them – like you ... only their profession differs.

Nice people. They were my friends ... and I was glad to be back among friends.

From them (eventually) I got a lead on Len.

I found him in a little shop, on a side street, way and gone to hell up the Edgware Road ... almost as far out as Burnt Oak.

He greeted me like a long-lost brother, then took me into the tiny workroom, at the rear, shifted some electronic gadgetry from a spare chair, then brewed instant coffee.

Maybe he knew why I'd called. Maybe he'd been marking time, waiting for me. If so, why not? ... we'd been a great team, and great teams rarely break up.

We sipped coffee and smoked cigarettes for a while. We brought ourselves up to date with each other. Len's wife had died, two years back, and his son and daughter were both married ... any week, now, he was due to be a grandfather. The shop was combined income and hobby; he took on work lesser experts wouldn't even touch – electric or electronic impossibilities which *he* made possible. The shop just about broke even, but the loot we'd salted away, in the good years, gave him occasional luxuries and (like me) the cops were satisfied he'd straightened out his own particular bend ... indeed, one of the local jack-sergeants was a hi-fi buff who brought all his problems of sound reproduction for Len to solve.

'Does it bore the hell out of you, Len?'

28

I made the question sound off-handed, as I held out the pack from which we were to take our second cigarettes.

He waited until we were both inhaling tobacco smoke before he answered.

He murmured, 'Andy, I wouldn't lie to you. You, of all people.'

'So?'

'Push the clock back twenty years. Even ten. I wouldn't be found dead in this damn place.'

I said, 'Age brings experience.'

'Yeah ... but you can't run as fast.'

'Did we ever run?' I asked, softly. 'Did we ever *have* to run?'

'No-o.' He smiled, wryly. 'But, if needed, we could have.'

'Meaning?' I urged.

'Andy, we were ... y'know.'

'The best?'

'Not many better.' His eyes had that faraway look that only comes with age and memories. The smile stayed, and he added, 'Why the hell didn't we move into Threadneedle Street? I sometimes think ... we *could* have.'

'If anybody,' I agreed.

We enjoyed the cigarettes, finished the coffee, and then I said, 'I need you, Len.'

He shook his head, sadly ... but didn't mean it.

'Rawle.' I dropped the name, as if it was an unclean thing.

'That shithouse.'

'The casinos ... you know about the casinos?'

'I heard.'

'The insurance gag. I needed protection ... I chose Rawle.'

'You're a mug, Andy. You surprise me.'

'I chose *him*.'

'You're still a mug.'

29

'Okay, I'm a mug,' I sighed. 'But now, Rawle wants a bust.'

'Not with me. Oh, no! Find some other...'

'There *isn't* another.'

He said, 'They're around ... if you look.'

'I don't *want* another.'

'Andy.' He pushed himself away from the bench, which he'd been using as a leaning-post, walked around the tiny room and waved the cigarette to emphasise what he was saying. 'Rawle ain't one of us. You know *that* ... I don't have to tell you what *Rawle* is. The only thing he can organise is pain. Pain ... that's his coinage, Andy. Pain, and the double-cross. The triple-cross. The double-double-cross. He couldn't play straight with his own mother. I've heard rumours. Some of 'em – y'know ... rumour always gets tarted up a little. But, even if they're only *half* right ... Rawle's pure psycho. He's killed ... that's what they say.'

'Believe them,' I said, solemnly.

'And you want *me* to tangle in with a bastard like *that*?'

I nodded.

'You must have holes in your head, Andy. I swear...'

'With me,' I interrupted.

'No! Not with the Scots Guards on my side. I wouldn't move within touching distance of a...'

'We can out-smart him,' I said.

He rested his backside on the bench again, looked down at me, with sorrow and disbelief in his eyes, and said, 'We don't work that way, son. We never did. We always worked clean. We always...'

'We never worked alongside a bastard like Rawle.'

'No ... thank Christ.'

'Len.' I was fighting for my life, and I knew it. I put a lot of honest urgency into my pleading. I said, 'How right you are. We never worked alongside a bastard like Rawle. We were smart, but clean. Proud. We were...'

'I'm still proud, Andy.'

30

'You're damn lucky.' I was losing ground, and the knowledge crept a hint of bitterness into my tone. 'I can't afford to be proud. The lolly – okay, I have that ... but I still can't afford to be proud.'

He watched my face, and what he saw brought wrinkles of sadness at his mouth corners, and between his eyes.

He said, 'Rawle?'

I nodded.

'He has you by the ear?'

'He has me by *everything*,' I said, disgustedly.

'I never thought I'd see the day,' he said, heavily.

I muttered, 'Yeah? Well ... this is the day.'

He hesitated then, in a gentle, probing tone, said, 'One job?'

'One job with Rawle,' I said.

'You – er – you sound as if there might be others.'

'I'm hungry for the old days,' I admitted gruffly.

'The excitement?' He smiled.

'The warm knowledge.'

'That we could beat anything?'

'Anything they thought up ... we always found a way round it.'

'But – er ...' He paused. 'Just the *one* job with Rawle?'

'Just the one.'

'With him? Or *for* him?'

It was a neat question. I thought around it for a few moments, then I said, '*For* him, I guess. I can't see Rawle sticking his neck out.'

'Not Rawle.' He drew on his cigarette, and his eyes narrowed as he concentrated his attention upon his thoughts. Then, he said, 'Okay, Andy ... one job *for* Rawle. Just the one. Maybe – maybe not ... but we might be able to draw his teeth. We've done it, before.'

'You're with me?' The question came out, with a sigh of relief.

'You need an alarm man.'

31

'That I do.'

'They may have thought up a few new tricks.'

'They always did.'

He said, 'Andy – I'm tempted ... but I'm older, now. Maybe not as cunning.'

'Risk it,' I urged, gently. 'We'll choose the jobs. Carefully. No more than half a dozen. A quick come-back ... then enough to live in comfort for the rest of our lives.'

'No more of this.' He glanced around the cluttered workroom with a wry look of distaste. 'The young pups who come here ... you wouldn't believe. Radio hams. Hi-fi buffs. Some – my Christ – they don't know positive from negative.'

'No more,' I promised.

'Okay.' He nodded. 'When ... and where?'

'I'll be in touch.'

He smiled a smile of gentle anticipation, and said, 'I'll be ready.'

We shook hands. The grip was firm, and it made me feel happier.

That was the day (when I got home) that the shock wave arrived. It was early evening, Anne was out – hotting it up with her buddies, somewhere – and the house was empty. No Muriel; nobody to give me the soft, sometimes sad-eyed, welcome-back-into-my-life routine.

Being married ... there must be an easier way for two people to share the same life.

Okay, forget the passion – the passion dies, like flames easing off to a steady glow ... it's what comes *after* the passion that takes some riding. It is not all hot drinking chocolate and slippers by the fire. It is not even a sharing of thoughts, because some of the thoughts are too personal – too involved – for any other living creature to understand. Show me a married man who denies having had day-dreams of being married to another woman, and I'll call him a liar to his face ... and, ninety-nine times out of every hundred, I'll be right. Life works that way. We all change, and the change is continuous; the man changes, the woman changes and, after twenty years, they are each bonded to a comparative stranger. And, from then on, kidology is the order of the day ... every day.

The peck on the cheek which passes off as a kiss. The terms of endearment, which are just so many words. And, at night, the counterfeit copulation; it isn't your wife you enter – it's some other woman ... maybe the dream creature you *might* have married. Jesus! The self-delusion. The trickery. The high moments, when the illusion borders upon reality ... when you truly *believe* you're making love to that elusive dream creature.

And – okay – what if you *were*? Wouldn't *she* be just as damn ordinary, after twenty years? Wouldn't you *still* be playing make-believe, in the dark?

That's marriage, friend.

Maybe it's the same for the women ... I wouldn't be surprised.

And yet, you go through the same old play-acting, day after day, week after week, until silver weddings, and golden weddings, and even diamond weddings notch themselves up on the calendar.

And, if that's the truth – and, with me, it *was* the truth – what drove me crazy when she broke the news about the Albert fink?

There is an answer to that, too.

Possession. Muriel was mine. Mine! Like the house in Putney, like the furniture that made the house into a home. Like the clothes on my back, and in my wardrobe. And this smooth-talking stranger had stolen her. He wasn't an adulterer ... he was a *thief*. Had he broken into my home, and attempted to steal my jacket, I'd have ripped the jacket to shreds, rather than let him have it.

Okay ... same thing.

33

But, then I wouldn't have had a jacket.

Now, I didn't have a wife ... same thing.

That evening, I sat alone, drank a little too much and tasted loneliness for the first time.

SIX ...

Then, I had trouble with Rawle.

Ten days, and he hadn't contacted me ... so I contacted *him*. He was back in that damn gymnasium of his, winding his legs like the clappers, and going nowhere, on the bicycle-machine. His face, arms and legs were rolling in sweat, and the gadget provided a well-oiled, off-stage whisper to our talk.

'We need to know,' I said.

'When I'm ready.'

'Look – nobody pulls a bust, blind ... not unless he's crazy.'

'And – hey, sweetie-boy – what's with the "we" talk?'

I was the expert, and there was only one way a gink like this could be unblinkered to the fact. I shot questions at him, like tennis balls from a serving machine and, when he'd stopped one, I gave him the next, before he'd time for any fancy stroke-play.

I said, 'You want a bust. Right?'

'That's why I did the favour. I ain't gonna ...'

'Safe, or vault?'

'You'll know, when I ...'

'*Safe, or vault?*'

'Hey, sweetie-boy, don't get ...'

'Which is it?' I snarled.

'Both.' He grinned a wolf grin as he broke the news. Maybe he thought the news would make my knees weak.

It didn't, and I snapped, 'Safe *inside* a vault. Right?'

'Inside a strongroom.'

'Which means underground, at a guess.'

'That's good guessing, sweetie-...'

'Alarmed?'

'I guess.'

'Open-circuit, or closed-circuit?'

'How the hell do I know? You're the...'

'What sort of alarms?'

'Alarms – what else? Cop-callers, like every other...'

'On the doors? On the locks?'

'How the hell do *I*...'

'On the walls? On the floors?'

'How the hell do *I* know? You're the...'

'You want it pulling, Rawle?'

'Sure I want it pulling. That's why...'

'Not just a quiet ride in a bogey-wagon?'

'Look – if you're as good as ...'

'I'm good, because I know my business.'

'Okay. So...'

'And, knowing my business means knowing what I'm up against.'

'As always, sweetie-boy. You're up against the cops. You're...'

'Wrong.'

'Uh?'

'I'm up against time, Rawle.'

'What the hell's that...'

'The time it takes the cops to reach out and grab.'

'So, that's what I...'

'But, they don't start reaching till the whistle blows.'

'I don't get the ...'

'And the whistle doesn't blow, until the alarm goes.'

'For Christ's sake. Even I...'

'So, I delay the whistle. Get it?'

'Yeah.' He stopped pedalling, wiped his face with a towel

35

which had been around his neck, then repeated, 'Yeah ...
okay.'

'Okay, what?'

'I'll get the set-up for you.'

'You'll get *nothing*,' I snapped.

'You've just been beefing about...'

I looked him in the eyes, and said, 'Would you believe
me, Rawle, if I told you I wouldn't believe *you*?'

'You talking in riddles, now?'

'I need to scan ... personally.'

'That ain't...'

'Otherwise, I risk one cell for another ... so, no deal.'

He eased his rump from the saddle of the bicycle-
machine and viewed me with narrowed eyes. Like I was a
cage-bird which had made a sudden, and unexpected, peck
at the finger which fed it. There was surprise and annoyance in the expression ... and just the hint of possible neck-
wringing.

He growled, 'You ain't *that* big, Martin.'

'I'm that clever. That careful.'

'No man tells me what to do, sweetie-boy.'

'Okay. But no man tells me how to do it.'

He used the towel on his face, again. It gave him time to
think. It also hid his eyes, and his expression.

Then, he said, 'Tomorrow.'

'Tomorrow, what?'

'You'll know where. You'll know what you're up
against.'

'And the bust?'

'I'll give you a week's notice.'

I pushed my luck another fraction, and said, 'One more
question.'

'I ain't gonna ...'

'Is it in Brum?'

'Uh?' He stared.

'Birmingham?'

'Why the hell should it be in ...'

'That's all I need, Rawle,' I interrupted. 'What time, tomorrow?'

He hesitated, before he grunted, 'Be ready at noon. You'll be picked up.'

It was a small victory, on my part – but a victory, nevertheless ... and I was satisfied.

Why the question about Birmingham?

We-ell, let me tell you. In all professions you need tools, and the tools of *my* profession aren't for sale over any Woolworth's counter. They are precision-made – indeed, the best are minor works of art – and they are hard to come by. They can be bought in London. They can be bought in the steel towns of Sheffield and Birmingham. They can be bought in few other places.

Of necessity, they are made, bought and sold quite illegally.

I, and a handful of others, know this, but, unfortunately, among that handful are included a few well-informed police officers. To buy at Birmingham and to *use* at Birmingham, therefore, would have woven a link – albeit a slender link ... but good coppers don't search for steel hawsers with which to entangle their quarry.

I allowed the Volvo to purr its way north, along the M.1, at its own comfortable cruising speed of sixty/sixty-five and, at the same time, allowed my mind to play tag with a first possibility.

We, who practise my skill, form a criminal aristocracy. We know each other, respect each other and, among ourselves, recognise each man's expertise. And one of our kind lived in Birmingham. He was good – probably not as good as I ... but, if not, only fractionally less skilled. Less than a year previously, he'd encountered an alarm system he hadn't been able to tame, and he was now in H.M. Prison,

Brixton. Rumour had it that the police had fallen short of the perfect arrest; that, despite the usual intensive search, his instruments hadn't been found.

His wife lived alone – waiting for his release – in the Castle Bromwich area ... and a loan would be safer than a sale.

I knew her slightly – we all 'know' each other ... *slightly*.

She was going to be my first port of call.

There was no false coyness. We were of a kind – of a class – and neither she, nor I, wasted time on pretence.

She asked me into the house – a neat, well-ordered, semi of the better-built kind – took my coat, and suggested that I stay for an evening meal. I accepted, without a second thought.

She said, 'The car?'

'It's in the drive.'

She smiled, and said, 'Use the garage, Mr Martin. The bogeys keep a collection. The descriptions of cars calling at this address.'

'Eager little beavers,' I murmured, then returned to the Volvo, and locked it safely out of sight, behind the up-and-over door of the garage which formed the end of the drive.

It was a nice meal. Shrimp cocktails, followed by a good mixed grill; cutlets, bacon, button mushrooms, sausages, kidneys and tomatoes.

As we ate, we talked and, again, there was no shyness; no awkwardness before either of us broached what might have been a semi-taboo subject.

'Is he going straight?' I asked.

'He says.' She smiled. 'They all say ... while they're inside.'

'And you?' She moved her shoulders slightly. 'What do you want him to do?'

'Whatever he wants.'

'It's a hell of a life,' I remarked.

'Ask your wife. She'll tell you.'

I swallowed, and said, 'She isn't with me any more.'

'Oh! I'm sorry.'

'Don't be. I'm not ... particularly.'

'Despite the fact that you *have* gone straight.'

'Temporarily.'

'Ah!'

'It wasn't that,' I explained hurriedly. 'She moved on, before I had a change of heart.'

'Probably she guessed.'

'I doubt it.'

'We are ...' With her fork, she doodled patterns in the film of fat on the bottom of her plate, as she spoke. 'We're an odd bunch, Mr Martin. The wives of professional criminals, I mean. We're in it for the glamour ... that's what we tell ourselves. That's why the rest of the world laughs at us. Feels sorry for us. Because, there *isn't* any glamour ... as if *we* didn't know. As if we're imbeciles, who don't even know when we're being hurt.'

'*Are* you hurt?' I asked.

'No. No more than any other person. Not by our husbands. We know what they are. If they're truthful – and most of them *are* truthful – we know what they are, before we marry them. I certainly did. I didn't try to change him ... few of us do. He was outside the law. That was one of the attractions. A bonus. The excitement ... the wild times we had, as a reward for the worry and the waiting.'

She allowed herself a quirky sort of smile. Sad, without being melancholy. Happy, without being joyful. But, above all else, quietly triumphant.

She said, 'I wouldn't change places. The wives of bank clerks. Of nine-to-five men. I wouldn't have *their* lives. They know – after the conviction, and the newspaper coverage – they all know. They're polite enough. Sym-

pathetic, even ... the real two-faced ones. But – y'know ...
they're jealous. Envious. I know. A woman can tell. They
wish *their* men had the guts.' She sighed, and ended, 'We
pay for everything, Mr Martin. Everybody. The solitude –
the being away from each other – that's only the payment. I
don't complain.'

We finished the meal in silence.

Maybe she was thinking about her husband.

Me? I was thinking about Muriel ... and (if this woman
was right) how bloody wrong I'd been.

We smoked cigarettes and sipped coffee, as I came to the
real reason for my visit.

I said, 'The police didn't find his kit.'

'No. They searched ... but they never found it.'

'I – er...'

'I know,' she interrupted, softly. 'You're back in business.'

'I don't know how good the kit is,' I fenced.

'He knew his trade.'

'That I'll grant you.'

'His tools never let him down.'

I smoked, drank coffee, and let her make the running.

She said, 'What happened to *your* kit?'

'I didn't hide it carefully enough.'

'Oh!'

'It happens, sometimes,' I said, sadly.

She stood up from her armchair and walked from the
room. I heard her climbing the stairs. I waited.

She was gone less than ten minutes and, when she
returned, she held out a zip-fastened, pigskin case, about six
inches long, four inches wide and two inches deep.

Without a word, I took the case, unzipped and opened
it.

They were the most beautifully manufactured set of picklocks I'd ever seen. Works of art, in surgical steel. Not just

40

so many skeleton keys – a skeleton key would have looked ugly and deformed in this company ... they were tools, warranted to tease open locks no mere skeleton key could hope to touch. Probes, with multiple 'steps', each of which could be raised, or lowered, to deal with each lever of a multiple-levered lock. Feelers, with hairpin fine antennae, with which to feel out the 'gates' and 'pockets' and 'bolt stumps'. Razor-thin dibbles and gouges, with which to screw up the workings of tumbler locks.

'Magnificent,' I breathed. 'Bloody magnificent.'

'Open it,' she suggested.

The case opened, like a book with a single page.

I turned the page, and my eyes widened, at the second assortment of goodies.

Diamond-tipped twist drills of tool-making steel. Ranging from hair-thin to three-sixteenths; capable of eating a hole into any lock-metal yet invented. And a couple of gadgets I didn't recognise.

'A battery-operated electric drill,' she explained, before I asked. 'It works off a pencil-torch battery. It has three speeds. The other thing.' She pointed. 'It fits at the base of the drill. A leather-covered pad, for the palm. To give whatever pressure you need.'

'Who...' I hesitated. I was about to ask the great unasked question. She wouldn't answer. If she knew the rules – and she certainly knew the rules – she wouldn't answer. Nevertheless, I *had* to ask the question. I said, 'Who made these beauties?'

'My father.' The answer came in a low, trusting tone. She said, 'There isn't another set like them, in the country.'

'In the *world*,' I emphasised.

'Probably.'

'Who made them?' I asked, again.

'My father. He was a craftsman.'

'You can say *that* again.'

'A watchmaker.'

41

'D'you think...' I moistened my lips, then tried the question, again. 'D'you think he'd make...'

'He's dead.' She killed the question, before it was born.
'Oh!'

I stroked the instruments, as they nestled in their velvet-lined housings. They were sweet to the touch; that tiny, battery-operated drill ... a masterpiece of miniaturised power – solid, despite its size, and obviously capable of slicing its way into metal tough enough to discourage drills ten times its size.

I breathed, 'Jesus ... no wonder he made damn sure they were well hidden.'

She lit a cigarette, and watched me fondle each instrument – each probe, each dibble – in turn, before returning it to its place in the case.

Is it possible to love inanimate objects? Is it possible to *fall* in love with them, on sight? I think it is and, *if* it is, I fell in love with that immaculate collection of illegal tools. My set had been good – better than most ... but this set made them clumsy, by comparison.

'Do you like them?' she asked, with a smile.

'*Like* them!' I couldn't drag my eyes from their perfection.

'They're being wasted,' she murmured.

'You mean ... You mean they're for *sale*?'

'No. Not for sale.'

'No.' I moved my lips in a tiny, wry smile. 'I thought that was too good to...'

'But they can be loaned, to the right man.'
'Oh!'

'Are *you* the right man, Mr Martin?' she asked, softly.

'I'm the man who'd value them, at their true worth.'

'And use them well?'

'Guaranteed.' The exchange – the possibilities which this kit promised – made me a little breathless.

'To be returned, of course,' she said.

'Naturally.'

'When asked for ... and no quibbles.'

'The day – the hour – they're asked for ... with no strings.'

'Not to be duplicated. *Never* to be duplicated ... used as a model.'

'Lady,' I said, with feeling, 'you know better. These *can't* be duplicated ... the man isn't born who *could*.'

She nodded, then said, 'That's the main part of the deal, then.'

'That...' I hardly dare ask the question. 'That I can *borrow* them? That I can *use* them?'

'For ten-per-cent of everything they lead you to.'

'It's a deal.' I gazed at the collection of superb breaking tools, and repeated, 'It's a deal. You have my word ... you can have it in writing.'

'No writing.' She smiled. 'You – my husband – you're the only class of thieves who still have honour. Your word's enough.'

I stayed the night. I shared her bed and, to those who don't know, that may seem a particularly *dis*honourable act.

Not so.

There are rules; very rigid rules but, at the same time, rules which accept human weaknesses and human feelings. I wasn't shacking up with her. I wasn't moving in. It wasn't a take-over. That made it acceptable; that she'd chosen, from the same level as her absent husband, and only for a one-night stand. This was allowed ... occasionally.

The rules are broken when a woman goes on the bash, while her man's inside. When she takes to the streets, when she has a 'regular' or when she entertains some Johnny-come-lately gigolo.

This wasn't the situation ... therefore, the rules weren't broken.

43

I was ready to go, when she said, quietly and without passion, 'Can you stay the night?'

I watched her eyes for a moment and, when they met mine without a flicker, I said, 'Yeah ... if you need me.'

She nodded, and said, 'That's why.'

So-o, it was okay.

It was okay ... and it was good.

We sipped booze, smoked cigarettes and watched the box until the programmes which interested us had all ended, then we climbed the stairs, bathed and climbed into bed, naked.

She'd waited. That was obvious, from the start. There was no finesse about her initial hunger for a man; she wasn't merely starved *of* sex, she was starving *for* sex. No words of endearment were exchanged ... we both knew they'd have been fancy lies, and what we were doing was, above all else, honest.

That first time was pure animal. She wrapped herself around me, drew me into her and went a little mad.

When it was over – when she was able to relax her clinging arms and legs – she rolled onto her back, stared at the ceiling, and breathed, 'God! That was good.'

The remark was not meant to be a compliment to me; a congratulatory utterance concerning either my virility or my expertise as a lover. It was more a sigh of relief. As if some drug had been administered, which had removed a long held pain.

We lay, side-by-side, for almost an hour. Silent, and each with our own thoughts.

Then, gradually, feeling came back to my loins and I rolled towards her and began to fondle her. She turned her head, smiled at me and murmured, 'Make this one night good enough for me to wait.'

I tried ... and she worked hard to help me.

We saw no sleep. We exhausted each other over and over again. There are tricks in love-making and, between us, I think we knew them all, and used them all. Modesty was a complete stranger, that night. We kept the lights blazing, and didn't give a damn. No erotic zone was left unexplored; no copulatory position was left untried.

We laughed, and we wrestled – we coupled, and we rested ... then we laughed, wrestled, coupled and rested, again. And, at dawn, I bathed, dressed and left.

She wore a négligée as she accompanied me to the hall and, just before I unlatched the door, she held out an oiled-silk-wrapped parcel.

She said, 'It was a four-man job, and they had the usual search. They found it ... and I want rid of it.'

I nodded, and said, 'Okay.'

I took the parcel.

I knew damn well what was inside the oiled-silk.

SEVEN...

The Morris was parked, and waiting, when I arrived back at Putney. As I opened the door of the Volvo, the rear door of the Morris also opened and a man stepped out and walked towards me.

He'd worn well; at first glance, he looked about half my age ... until the range was close enough to see the web of tiny wrinkles around the eye and mouth corners. He was smartly, but quietly, dressed. He had that assurance which only comes with real authority. And, he looked annoyed.

As I locked the Volvo, he snapped, 'We've been waiting.'

'It's not illegal,' I cracked, as I tested the door.

'Where the hell have you been?'

I straightened, eyed him, then said, 'I've been where I've just come from, mac. That's the truth. Ask any more questions, and you get lies.'

'I expected you to be ready. Waiting.'

45

'*You* did?'

'That's why...'

I snapped, 'Before we go any further, who's the feed?'

'What's that?'

'The cross-talk routine. I'm the comic ... who's the feed?'

'Watch it, Martin,' he warned. 'Rawle doesn't like...'

'You from Rawle?'

'You know damn well...'

'Nothing,' I snapped. 'Except that you talk like a character from a badly-written Hank Janson.'

His nostrils quivered. He was unused to insults. Big deal – I didn't like him ... so, he'd better *get* used to insults.

I took the first stride in my walk to the house, and he caught my shoulder. I did a smart pivot, until I was facing him, then kneed him in the knackers. It hurt him, and it surprised him ... maybe he thought Putney didn't permit ungentlemanly conduct.

I continued my walk to the house, and he caught up with me at the front door.

He said, 'Martin, if I...'

'Keep your hands to yourself, creep,' I snarled. 'And fix your watch. The time was noon ... you're much too early.'

'Rawle said...'

'Rawle said noon. I *agreed* noon. Until then, go round a corner, somewhere, and screw yourself.'

I closed the door in his face, hung my driving coat on a hall peg and walked into the main room. I flopped into an armchair and untied the string around the oiled-silk parcel. I guessed what I'd find, and I was right. A shooter; a thirty-eight Colt 'Agent' revolver; a six-shot, snub-nosed piece of very lethal ironmongery. It was loaded, and there was a box of re-loads included in the parcel.

She'd said it had come from 'the usual search' and this, too, I both understood and went along with.

The genuine peterman – the safe-breaker who takes a

46

personal pride in pitting his wits against those of the safe-makers – doesn't need a gun. Guns are for yobs; for the G.B.H. crowd, the blag boys and the boot clique. Fire a gun at a safe, and what happens? ... you end up with a lot of noise, and a safe that's still laughing at you. The only thing a gun does is add time, if you're caught.

So-o, when a pro steers a job, there's always a search. The last thing; at the final rendezvous, and just before they get into the cars for the scene. The boss-man searches everybody, then cards are cut to see who (in turn) searches the boss-man. (The card-cutting thing cuts out any previously arranged fiddle.) And any shooters, or knives, or coshes or brass-knuckles – or *any* damn thing the bogeys might tag as an 'offensive weapon' – are ousted, and left behind. And, why? Because the law does a big tut-tut whenever 'offensive weapons' are linked in with a straight lift; the indictment includes some very emotive words, and the lagging, when it arrives, is heavy enough to discourage permafrost.

Hence the Colt.

The search which had unearthed that Colt had halved the slam time of every man on the job.

'Bang-bang toys, now. You're suddenly getting gutsy. Where's the catch?'

My beloved daughter had arrived, unannounced (and unheard) and was showing off her gold-plated vocabulary.

'Cut it out,' I sighed. 'Every time you open your damn mouth I worry about the money it's cost to teach you those long words.'

'Mother hasn't arrived in America.'

She said it as she collapsed into a relaxed heap in another armchair.

I didn't drop the gun, or hit the ceiling, or do handstands ... or anything like that. I just held my breath for about five seconds, and wished my heart would hurry back to its regular beat.

She said, 'I was worried.'

'Yeah?' I breathed.

'She said she'd write. I phoned the school, and there's been no letters. So, I phoned Albert.'

'France and America?' I croaked.

'Where else?'

'Why not the moon? You don't pay the phone bill.'

'She hasn't *arrived*,' she said, angrily.

'So?' I was getting my confidence back.

'So, where the hell is she?'

'Maybe she's another "Albert" tucked away, somewhere.'

'You're a slob. D'you know that, slob? ... you're a slob.'

'I know now,' I assured her.

'What's the next move, slob?' she asked.

'Get rid of the damn thing.'

'What?' She stared.

'The gun. I don't believe ...'

'I'm talking about mother, slob,' she snapped.

'Hey, honey.' I hung warning lights around my tone. 'Any more yap about my social status, and you have my word ... I'll pan your fanny till you'll need to stand upright for the rest of the day.'

'Big man,' she sneered.

'Yeah. Big enough to give a very lippy daughter one hell of a thrashing ... and slob enough to do just that.'

Inside her nutty little brain, the certainty that I wasn't kidding clicked into place and, for a moment, she looked sulky.

Then, she bounced back to normal, and said, 'What about mother?'

'What about her?' I countered.

'Where the hell is she?'

'I don't know. Nor do I care.' I spoke the words in all honesty.

'Something could have happened to her.'

'That I should be so lucky,' I murmured.

'Albert's worried.'

'Great. That makes my day.'

'He says he'll give her another week.'

'Then what? Some other frustrated wife? Does he have a list?'

'Then,' she said, 'he's coming over.'

'Here?' There was the ghost of a wobble to my voice.

'Sure ... to find out what's happened.'

I stood up from the chair; I forced the muscles of my legs to lift me, and hold me steady. My mind raced, like a runaway pin-wheel figuring out the right things to say.

There weren't any right things to say, so I settled for, 'Is that so?'

'*He'll* find out,' she said, confidently.

It was the way she said it. The certainty. The matter-of-fact positiveness.

I walked towards the window, and said, 'What is he? Some sort of miracle-man?'

'Of a sort.'

'Yeah?' The Morris was still parked out front.

'He's a Pinkerton man.'

'A – a ...'

'The Pinkerton Agency. He's one of their operatives.'

'I know what the Pinkerton Agency is,' I breathed. 'I'm not *that* big a slob.'

Who the hell doesn't? Who the hell *doesn't* know what the Pinkerton Agency is?

'The Ever Open Eye' – that's their trade-mark – and, from it, the name 'private eye' ... filched and used by every ten-a-penny unofficial investigation outfit in the world.

Old Ma Fate kicked hard-working crooks in the teeth when she brought that Glaswegian Chartist into the world. Having bent the laws of his own country, he belted off to the New World and, very niftily, changed horses in midstream. In 1850 Chicago, he established Pinkerton's

49

National Detective Agency; just about the only straight law-enforcement outfit in Uncle Sam Land at that time. He hounded some of the big names in western folk-lore, and notched *their* deaths on the gun-butts of *his* operatives ... and, from then on, there was no stopping him. He ran the secret service division of the national army, in Virginia, by 1861, and why? ... because, until Hoover knocked the F.B.I. into shape, Pinkerton was just about the only police circus wholly trustworthy.

A fantastic outfit. Was then – still is ... and Muriel had to play footsie with one of *their* operatives!

I left my darling daughter, and went upstairs to change and to ponder upon the cockeyed spin of this lunatic world.

The phone rang and, when I lifted the receiver, I heard the not-so-dulcet tones of my lord and master, Rawle.

Rawle rasped, 'What's the big idea, Martin?'

I saw no good reason to make-believe he'd cornered the market in bad tempers, so I rasped back, 'You tell *me* ... then I'll tell *you*.'

'My boys are wasting time.'

'So, what? I don't meet their pay cheque.'

'You wanna see the place, Martin?'

'I'm *going* to see the place, Rawle. We take that for granted.'

'So, beat it. Let 'em take you.'

'What the hell ...'

'*Now*, Martin. Drop that phone, and get out there.'

'Rawle,' I snarled, 'your racket may not take too much account of time. A day here, a week there. But *mine* works by the second ... and it's habit-forming.'

'They can't wait for noon.'

'I wasn't told.'

'I'm telling you *now*, sweetie-boy.'

'Noon,' I snapped.

'Who the hell d'you think ...'

'I'm talking to you, Rawle ... if that's what you were going to ask.'

'You could be breathing borrowed air, Martin,' he choked.

'It's still noon.'

'Martin, what the hell's eating you?'

'You don't trust me, Rawle. That's what's eating me ... among other things.'

'The hell I don't! I send a car ...'

'Three hours ahead of time.'

'So?'

'Just to check the cops haven't binoculars at the ready.'

'Who said that?'

'Rawle,' I said, heavily, 'the dew might have been thick, this morning ... but I wasn't with it.'

There was a moment's silence, then he said, 'I have to protect my interests, Martin. That follows.'

'From me?'

'From everybody, sweetie-boy. That's why I live good.'

I said, 'Okay. Protect your interests till noon, then take a chance,' and hung up, before he could reply.

Rawle. I was pig-sick of Rawle and his devious ways. Maybe muscle needed this sort of round-the-corner tactics, but I wasn't selling muscle. I was selling something Rawle didn't know the meaning of. Pride. Craft. Oneupmanship, with a stretch behind high walls as a forfeit if you lost the game.

And now, this damn Pinkerton worry ...

I shoved Rawle and Pinkerton to one side of my mind, picked up the phone and telephoned Len's number.

He answered, and I said, 'Andy here. You still got that camera, Len?'

'The miniature?'

'Yeah.'

'Sure. Why?'

'Filmed?' I asked.

'Loaded,' he replied.

'A favour,' I said. 'Wrap it up, neatly. Then deliver it to the manager of my Hammersmith place, before noon. Tell him I'll be collecting it.'

'Can do.' He paused, then asked, 'Things moving, Andy?'

I said, 'Today, I take pictures. Tonight, we see what we're up against.'

'Boy!' he breathed.

'Have the developing gear ready.'

'Ready, and waiting.' I could almost feel the grin, all the way along the telephone wire.

I dressed neatly and, over my suit, I used a loose-fitting, lightweight mac. Unbelted. I thought about it – had second thoughts ... then decided to have third thoughts. I slipped the Colt into the pocket of the mac. Just in case.

I was no gunman... but the apes with whom I was due to keep company weren't going to be friendly and, to them, being unfriendly was another way of saying 'being physical'. That little snub-nosed thirty-eight could be the equaliser, if they decided to be boisterous.

At noon – *exactly* – I opened the door, and walked to the waiting Morris.

EIGHT...

Counting the driver, three of Rawle's frighteners had been sent as escort. The driver ... presumably, because he could drive a motor car. The goon whose goolies I'd hurt ... presumably, because he was supposed to have brains hiding somewhere under his hair. And, the original Laughing Boy ... presumably, to prove that the Neanderthal Man was still alive and kicking.

A great trio!

As I climbed into the back of the Morris, I said, 'First stop, the casino. Hammersmith.'

The boy with the aching testicles turned, in the front passenger seat, and said, 'Rawle gave orders that...'

'I don't give a monkey's what Rawle ordered.' I closed the door, and settled back, alongside ape-face. 'I've talked with Rawle. You do what *I* say. Hammersmith.'

Get it?

With the complete yob, it always works. Use the right tone of voice; the parade-ground bite, with no hooks upon which to hang arguments. Tart up the truth; make it sound like something it isn't, and work the con that suggests that that something originated from where it just *might* have originated. It works, every time. The bully-boys are not paid to think (supposing they even possess the necessary equipment) ... they are paid to obey orders. Okay – slam an order at their kissers ... they act like so many robots.

Hammersmith it was.

I nipped out of the Morris and, sure enough, Len had delivered the goods. When I climbed back into the car, I had a camera.

That camera.

Let me tell you...

If it's miniaturisation you want, stick with the Japanese. They have all the know-how, plus a gift nobody else seems to possess. They are also working their nuts off, ridding themselves of the once-upon-a-time 'Made in Japan' image.

That camera was made in Japan. It was made by an off-shoot of the Sansui organisation, before Sansui began its all-out bid for sound equipment. Could be, you can still buy such a camera, over the counter – second-hand – in the streets of Tokyo ... but, I doubt it. Certain it is you can't buy one on the open market anywhere else in the world.

It was made for a purpose; to take photographs, where

photographing is strictly forbidden. Its shape was that of a slim matchbox, and its lens was a work of art; wide-angled and with a general focus which missed nothing up to twenty yards. It was button-operated, and a single press of the button took the picture, and moved the spool onto the next frame. As simple as *that*. Eighty frames per spool ... and each frame clear-cut enough to take a blow-up large enough to show the individual whiskers in a man's moustache.

That was the camera, and that camera was going to show Len and I exactly what we were up against.

I stripped it of its wrapping, before I left the casino and, when I climbed back into the car, the camera was neatly palmed in my right hand, and ready for use.

We moved north-east – through Paddington, Islington and Hackney – across the marshes and up through Epping Forest, then I lost the route, somewhere between Chingford and Woodford. We hit the minor roads, and back streets; maybe deliberately, as a means of throwing me off course ... Rawle had a mind like that, and the goon at the wheel would obey orders to the last right turn.

We stopped near the mouth of a cul-de-sac and, ahead of the windscreen – about fifty yards farther along what was some brand of second-class high street – was a parade of shops; the usual ten, or dozen, wide-windowed emporiums, with a tar-mac frontage separating their entrances from the pavement. A drug store, a bank, a small, self-service dump, a butcher ... the normal collection.

The goon with what passed as brains under his bonnet, half turned in the front seat.

He said, 'Your name's Smith...'

'That's interesting,' I murmured. 'All this time, and I didn't know.'

'Listen, Martin ... your name's *Smith*. There's a punk outside the bank. He's waiting for you. His name's Jones ...'

'Where the hell do you pick these names from? Out of a hat?'

'His name's Jones,' he repeated, in a tight voice. 'Young guy. Grey suit. He'll be carrying a copy of *The Spectator*...'

'Not a red carnation in his buttonhole?' I mocked.

'Hey, Martin ... cut the funnies, and listen. *The Spectator* ... get it? He's waiting for you. Introductions ... then, follow his lead. He'll take you. You're an expert in filigree gold-work, and he wants your advice. Get it?'

I nodded.

'Don't arse it up ... eh?' he said.

I smiled, and said, 'With you boys around *I* don't even have to try.'

'Okay, we'll be waiting.' He jerked his head in the general direction of the cul-de-sac. 'Round the corner, in the dead-end.'

I climbed from the Morris, slid the mac from my shoulders and draped it over my left arm. The camera was hidden in my left hand, and I started taking pictures.

The boy in the grey suit was young ... and scared. He held *The Spectator*, like he was doing a T.V. ad for that publication. His heels left the tar-mac, with a jerk, as I spoke.

I said, 'Mr Jones? My name's Smith. It's a small world.'

'Eh?' He blinked, and shied, like a startled horse.

'We have some filigree work to examine,' I said.

'Oh – er – yes ... quite.'

And that was my first big surprise. The voice ... it had 'public school' stamped on every drawled vowel. I did a quick, mental reappraisal of friend Rawle. Bouncers he handled ... but other things, too. This one, for example. Pure cut-glass and silver cigarette-case. And even *he* was one of Rawle's pigeons.

He murmured, 'If you don't mind accompanying me, Smith.'

'Not at all ... *Jones*.'

We didn't go into the bank – and that was my second big surprise – but, instead, we strolled the length of the parade of shops, turned left, into a slightly crummy offshoot street, which ran parallel with the cul-de-sac then, with a ping of an old-fashioned door-bell, entered a jeweller's shop.

And, all the time – every few strides – I was taking pictures.

It was a jeweller's shop. You've seen them. They don't have eye-catching sites, in pedestrian precincts; they hide, as unobtrusively as possible, in the darkest corners they can find. They have no neon-lit display cabinets; no extra, and cunningly positioned, illumination meant to emphasise the sparkle of the goods for sale. The rocks *these* shops handle provide their own, inner illumination.

It was one of those sort of shops.

And it was run by a kibbutzin-wallah. A real, one-hundred-per, four-by-two ... conk, skull-cap, waving palms, and all.

As he came from behind the counter, he bent his lips into a smile of greeting, spread his hands, and said, 'Haye, Captain Jones. It's good to see you, again. It ain't too often we get a customer, like yourself, Captain Jones. It's a pleasure to do business with you.'

Jones? *Captain* Jones? We-ell – I guess some people *are* called Jones ... and, maybe a few hold commissioned rank.

Jones said, 'Mr Noble, this is my friend ... Mr Smith.'

'Any friend of Captain Jones is a friend of mine, Mr Smith. Maybe I could interest you in something good, but not too expensive. A watch, maybe. Cufflinks, maybe.'

Before I could say anything, Jones drawled, 'Actually ... it's about the pendant I'm interested in.'

'The pendant ... why not? It's a good pendant. Would I give rubbish room-space in this place? Ain't I got enough trouble selling good stuff, without wasting room with rubbish?'

Jones said, 'Mr Smith specialises in filigree work.'

'Ain't that nice, eh? Now you're gonna *really* learn about that pendant.'

'If we might see it, please.'

'Sure. Mind the steps, that's all. Like I told you, last time, they ain't safe. But builders ... who wants to do building repairs these days? Everybody does it yourself. Me? I ain't been trained to saw wood ... at my age, should I learn? So – like I say – mind the steps. Y'see, Mr Smith – maybe Captain Jones mentioned – it don't do to keep the good stuff where some young hooligan can knock me over the head and take it. The world ain't fit to live in, no more. It ain't safe, no more. This way, I maybe get a crack on the head ... but that's all. That I should get a crack over the head, that's bad enough. But that I should also lose some of my best stuff. That's crazy ...'

It was the usual Yid monologue, and he led the way to the back of the shop, and down the stairs. And, all the time, the old camera was recording things. The light could have been better, but the film was super-sensitive ... so, I hoped for the best.

The shop might not have been much but, downstairs in the basement, the crown jewels would have felt at home.

The door was built to stop a rhino charge ... with a lock to match. And, beyond the door – about four yards along a very solid-looking passage – an equally solid-looking steel-barred gate led into the strong-room.

Unlike the shop, the strong-room was well-lit. The safes – three of them – filled one wall-space. In the middle of the room, under a low-slung lamp, there was a velvet-topped table.

The Jew-boy locked the gate, then said, 'It ain't that I don't trust you, Captain Jones. And – Mr Smith – it ain't that I don't think you're an honest man. But – y'know – people talk. All the time, people talk. Even in their sleep. So, I ain't gonna apologise when I ask you not to watch

57

what's in the safe, see? Why should you be interested? You're both good business-men. You understand these things.'

We turned our backs to him as he shuffled to the middle safe.

So, what? ... I'd taken four snapshots of those three beauties, already. And, while we had our back to him, he had his back to us, which meant I could get every detail of that strongroom – floor, ceiling and walls – on prints a dozen times, without him knowing.

After that, it was pure gaff.

The pendant was good. Twenty-two carat, and with the Chester impress of the two-leaved acorn ... which meant it had been imported, and certified by that corporation. The filigree work was good; I'd seen better ... but not much better, and not often. I handled it, like I figured an expert might handle it. I made vague noises with my mouth, like I figured an expert might make.

And, when the Jones boy asked me a question with his eyes, I said, 'It's good. It's very good.'

'Show me a better,' said the Jew-boy.

After that, it was up to Jones.

He played it off the top of his head. He wasn't going to buy the damn thing, but he had to leave things in the air. He drawled sweet nothings for about ten minutes, then promised to come back with a firm decision, within the week.

Once more, we turned our backs – and I pressed a few more snaps off – the Jew-boy unlocked the gate, then the door, and we returned upstairs.

Five minutes later, I was back in the Morris.

Nobody asked questions. The ride to Regent's Park was both quick and quiet. Iron Man opened the door of Rawle's pad, and I followed him into the library.

Library!

At a guess, Rawle bought his books by the yard, to fill the empty spaces on the shelves, and because the bindings went with the colour scheme. Maybe he *could* read – I don't have positive proof to the contrary – but, sure as hell isn't an ice factory, he hadn't read *them*.

He was in a swivel-chair, behind a near-antique desk and, when his personal bouncer had left, he looked at me, and said, 'Well?'

'I liked the pendant,' I said.

I dropped into a convenient chair, and draped my mac over one knee. The camera and the Colt were in the pockets of the mac; I didn't want Rawle to know about one, and I felt bigger, and safer, while I could feel the weight of the other.

Rawle smiled, and the smile gave the lie to the egg-heads who work out stupid and useless facts ... that the human animal is the only animal on earth which shows its teeth, except in anger. Rawle was angry; or, if not, close enough to anger to need no more than a tiny nudge. I'd blown him a few raspberries, that day, and made him swallow every one. That he was neither used to the taste, nor prepared to *get* used to the taste, showed in his eyes, his expression and even in his smile.

'Sweetie-boy,' he purred, 'you didn't go just to glim the pendant.'

'Nevertheless, it *was* a nice pendant,' I insisted.

'The safe?'

'Three safes,' I corrected him.

'The vault?'

'A strongroom. As strong as most ... stronger than many.'

'Can you crack it?' he asked.

'The strongroom? The safe? Or, all three safes?'

'Is that a choice?' he sneered.

'Yeah.' I nodded. 'Given time – the right equipment, and men who do what *I* say – you can have the full house.'

59

'Is that a fact?' His eyes widened a little, and some of the anger eased itself out of his eyes.

'Given time,' I repeated.

'Which means?'

'Days. Probably weeks.'

'And that,' he said, gruffly, 'you ain't got.'

'How much time?' I pressed. Before he could answer, I added, 'And, Rawle, don't make it hours ... otherwise, you're pissing in the wind.'

'Days,' he said, softly.

'How many?'

'Ten.'

'It's possible,' I conceded.

'*Make* it possible, Martin.'

'No threats, Rawle,' I murmured. 'You need me. I'm the one thing you're very light on ... ability. Talent. Finesse.'

'You love yourself, sweetie-boy.'

'I don't short-change myself ... if that's the same thing.'

'Okay.' He let the two syllables ride out slowly, and astride a deep – almost resigned – tone. 'We had a deal. I kept my half.'

I said, 'I'll keep mine. But *my* way.'

'Which means?'

I gave him the complete picture, in a few words.

I said, 'I can handle the safes. We have to go in through the wall, if possible. Through the shop – through the two doors – that's asking for trouble ... anything could be wired, on the way. I can handle the safes ... but I've to *get* to the safes. That means a first class alarm man. I have one. He's standing by.'

'The hell he is! Who else have you...'

'We're a team, Rawle. Long established. I didn't whistle him out of the nearest four-ale bar.'

He took a deep breath, then said, 'Okay. You have an alarm man. What else?'

'I'll let you know.'

'Eh?'

'Tomorrow. Twenty-four hours from now ... at my place.'

'I don't pay social calls on ...'

'This time, you break the habit, Rawle.'

'Why the hell not *here*? What's wrong with ...'

'Remember Nixon?' I chuckled.

'Who?'

'Nixon ... ex-President.'

'What the hell's that ...'

'He bugged the White House. Top to bottom. Back to front.'

'So?'

'There's only one place on God's earth I *know* isn't bugged. That's where we talk business ... from here, on.'

'This place ain't wired, Martin. Why the hell should I ...'

As I stood up from the chair, I said, 'Why the hell should *anybody*, Rawle? But, they do. It's that sort of world.'

NINE...

That night, we turned back the clock. Len and I. We returned pages to the calendar – whole years of pages – and became young again as we watched the screen upon which we projected blow-ups from the frames I'd taken that afternoon.

The safes...

I said, 'Good safes. Chubb TDR metal. Anti-explosive bolts ... but, we aren't going to blow it, so they don't matter.'

'But, TDR ... that's tough, Andy.' Len made the observation, *as* an observation. Not as an expression of doubt.

'Torch and drill resisting,' I mused.

'Yeah. I know. And...'

'About on a par with the Chatwood-Milner Duplextra metal.'

'Agreed. I merely mention the fact ... that it's tough.'

'Yesterday,' I said, dreamily, 'I was given a new toy. *Loaned* it, actually. It includes a *very* portable drill. Three-speed ... including very high-speed. And, with it, a set of diamond-tipped, tungsten-carbide bits. We've worked TDR metal, in the past, Len ... we'll *play* with it, this time.'

Len blew a soft whistle, then said, 'So-o, no ring-saw.'

'Ring-saw be damned.' I almost laughed outright, at the memory. 'Remember the last time we tackled TDR with a ring-saw? It chewed seven, to hell, before we had the hole there.'

'Eight,' he corrected me.

'Eight? Was it eight?'

He chuckled, 'We damn near spent as much on ring-saws as we lifted.'

'But, not this time, mate,' I promised. 'This time, just the lock. A few well-placed holes. A tickle here, a nudge there, and we're in.'

'How long for each safe?'

'Fifteen minutes ... about.'

'Make it an hour for the three – double it, to cover emergencies ... say, two hours on the safes.'

'If we take all three,' I said.

'Why not?'

'Rawle fingered the centre one. Whatever it is he wants, it's in *that* safe.'

'So-o, whatever he *doesn't* want, is ours. Plus whatever we find in the other two ... why not?'

I was staring at the screen, and I mused, 'Y'know, Len, it's a little screwy. Those safes. They're hellish *good* safes. And that vault. Why?'

'Why, what?'

'That jeweller's. Okay – it was above-average ... but *those* safes. And the strongroom-cum-vault. What the hell does he keep down there?'

'We'll know, Andy. Soon. Try the next picture.'

I pressed the knob, then pressed it a second time, as the first press merely showed the back of the jeweller, as he opened the heavy door of the strongroom. The second shot showed a corner of the strongroom.

Len said, 'No ... back one.'

'It's the entrance, that's all. The door ...'

'I know. That's what I want to see.'

I clicked the projector back to the rear of the jeweller.

'There! See it?' Len leaned forward in his chair.

'What?'

'Towards the top of the jamb. About six inches down, at a guess ... just above his shoulder.'

Those eyes of his were sharp. I'd missed it.

I breathed, 'Christ! A recessed micro-switch ... right?'

'Right,' he agreed, softly. 'Which means – which *must* mean – the whole damn room's wired.'

'No contact mats,' I said, with certainty. 'Solid concrete floor. I'll stake my life on *that*.'

'Okay – no contact mats ... I'll take your word. But that's a micro-switch, if I ever saw one. Five gets you ten, there's another on that gate arrangement ... and my money says the whole room's wired.'

'For Christ's sake!'

'I dunno why, Andy. We'll answer that question when we're inside. But, let's go over those pictures again. One at a time, and very slowly.'

We did, too. It took us three hours – a little longer – but, by the end of the stint we knew what we were up against.

What I couldn't get – what neither of us could get – was *why*? A Jewish jeweller – so what? ... they're ten a penny. Every kibitzer figures he knows all there is to know about stones, and some even do. They set up shop. Some cheap.

63

Some pricey. Some straight. Some bent. Some take-your-pick. They're like the rest of the world ... and the rest of the world doesn't figure it owns the Koh-i-noor's twin sister, plus its parents, grandparents and half a dozen uncles thrown in for good measure. And *that* is the size of the glitter deserving of all that sophisticated safety-first garbage.

We turned on the lights, allowed the projector to cool down and sipped iced beer. And we thought, and we thought, and we thought ... and it still didn't make sense.

Len ticked them off on his fingers.

'Micro-switches, on the vault doors. That means the whole works – the full alarm system. Closed circuit, double-pole wiring in the walls ... bet on it. Those eye-pieces, about knee-high, let into the wall ... photo-electric, infra-red. That circular gewgaw, on the wall, above the safes – the diaphragm holder ... differential air pressure alarm. Double-checked, by the classy fan in one corner of the ceiling. Then – when we weave our way through *that* jungle – Chubb TDR safes. What the hell's *in* there, Andy? What the hell *deserves* all that security?'

'Something,' I growled. 'Something very important – very important to Rawle ... and something the insurance people wouldn't touch.'

'That, for sure.'

'So-o ... not gems.'

'Hot gems?' he suggested.

'I don't buy it,' I said.

'No. Nor do I. It was just a thought. But, what the hell else?'

'I dunno.' I tipped what was left of my beer down my throat, and said, 'But, tomorrow, I ask Rawle.'

TEN...

We were back in the gymnasium, again. I was worried – curious and intrigued – and even worried enough to back down from my tough-talk of the day before. I was calling on Rawle. I was backing down from yesterday's my-place-or-nowhere ultimatum, and I expected contempt from the big bastard, but that wasn't what I was getting.

Rawle didn't give me contempt.

Instead, he leaned against the weight-lifting-machine, wearing white shorts and sweat shirt, and talked as if to a slightly misguided son.

He said, 'Look – Martin – I did you a small favour ... right?'

'Right.' I nodded.

'I mean – let's not kid ourselves, sweetie-boy ... you cooled your old woman. But good.'

'That's past. That's ...'

'It ain't past, Martin. It ain't past, because you still owe me the favour ... right?'

'To get into the safe?'

'Right.'

'I'll do it ... don't worry.'

'So, where's the beef? We're both happy.'

'*I'm* not happy,' I said, bluntly.

'For why?' He plucked a cigar from the breast pocket of the sweat shirt, and began to strip it of its cover of cellophane.

'I want to know what I'm after.'

'Inside the safe?' He was stalling for time and, if he was trying to hide that fact, he was making a lousy job of it.

'Inside the safe,' I assured him. 'Which is inside a strong-

65

room geared to fire rockets and sound hooters, if as much as a stray mosquito finds airspace inside its walls. Just what the hell does Noble keep in those safes?'

'Noble?' He looked perplexed.

'It's his shop,' I reminded him.

'Oh – yeah ... Noble.'

Do you ever get that feeling? That you're blind? That you're walking forward – slowly, and with your arms outstretched for obstacles – and that your fingers have touched something particularly nasty ... but you can't yet put a name to it?

I watched him shove the cigar into his mouth, and I watched him light it, with a fancy lighter he'd fished from the pocket of his shorts. It was an eyeball-to-eyeball thing ... and he blinked, before I did.

'It – er – it ain't important,' he muttered.

'What?'

'There's a deed box.'

'Inside one of the safes?'

'Yeah.'

'The middle safe?'

'Yeah ... I think.'

'Inside that strongroom?'

'Yeah.'

'You're not tough any more, Rawle,' I observed, mildly.

'Eh?'

'That thing – inside the deed box – whatever it is ... it moves mountains. *Your* mountain.'

'I want it,' he said, flatly.

'What is it?' I asked.

He shook his head. A little jerkily, and with a touch of panic.

'And, if I say I don't move, until I know?'

He breathed a hunk of cigar smoke, exhaled, then pushed himself clear of the weight-lifting-machine.

He said, 'Stick around, Martin. I'll be back ... then I'll show you something.'

I drove the Volvo, while Rawle told me which turnings to take. Just the two of us and, apart from the directions, no talk.

We went east, along the north bank of the river; towards Stepney, Limehouse, Poplar; into warehouse-land.

I stopped, when he told me to stop, parked and locked the Volvo and, from there, we walked. The streets were like canyons, between the walls of the warehouses. Narrow, mean streets, where nobody lived; the haunt of cats, rats and stray dogs; the arse-end of a major port.

He unlocked the side door of a warehouse, and I followed him inside. It wasn't quite empty ... but it was a hell of a long way from being full. It had packing cases, crates, a lot of floor space and a lot of echoes.

We climbed two sets of stairs. To the second floor.

He stopped at the door of a partitioned corner; a big, solid-looking door, with a good lock and a bar-handled latch, top and bottom.

He unlocked the door, yanked on the bar handles and hauled the door open ... and the cold hit me, like an arctic blast.

He flicked a switch, and the inside was flooded with light.

A walk-in deep-freeze. Meant for meat. The walls glittered with white frost. The rails and hooks were empty ... all except one hook.

Meant for meat ... and one hook *held* meat!

The sight of her sent me light-headed. Damn near knocked me out. The stab wounds. The staring eyes. The gaping mouth. Her slashed clothes. Everything filmed with the thin film of frost.

The opening of the door had caused some sort of draught, and she swung, gently, on the hook ... and I wanted to puke.

He closed the door, slammed the latch handles back into position, then turned the key in the lock.

As if to round everything off – to complete the circle – he murmured, 'We also have the knife ... dabs and everything.'

I nodded. I still wanted to puke.

We walked back to the Volvo, in silence. I was busy – too busy to talk ... too busy making myself *believe* it.

I drove him back to Regent's Park, without having to be told directions.

Somewhere near Holborn, he said, 'You'll get me that deed box, Martin ... right?'

I croaked, 'Yeah. I'll get you the deed box.'

And that was it ... what else?

I didn't go back to Putney, after I'd dropped Rawle. Hell knows why, but I went straight on to Len's place. Maybe I wanted to reassure myself; that *clean* crooks still inhabited the earth.

I wobbled a little, as I entered the shop.

Len came towards me, cupped my elbow in his hand, and said, 'Andy. What the hell ...'

'Okay ... it's okay,' I choked, but allowed him to lead me into the workroom, at the back, and ease me onto a chair.

He fussed around, like an old hen; a nice guy, worried because his buddy was off-balance. He locked the shop, brewed tea – hot, strong, sweet tea, laced with brandy – and, while the tea was brewing, he lighted a cigarette and placed it between my trembling fingers.

(... and she swung there ... the hook bedded into the nape of her neck ... tiny ice crystals, on her lashes ... her eyes wide and frozen...)

I dived for the door at the rear of the workroom, opened it and spewed my guts all over the flagstones of a tiny, walled yard.

I staggered back to the chair, folded myself into it and mumbled some sort of apology. I felt better for the puke ... weak as a starved kitten, but better.

'You – er – you need a doctor?' asked Len, anxiously.

I shook my head. I even managed the ghost of a wry grin.

That's what friends are for. To be anxious, but not to ask the wrong questions. To know what to do but, more than that, to know what *not* to do.

Len handed me the beaker of tea, before he joined me in the cigarette stakes. I sipped at the tea, then took a good mouthful, and the brandy restored some of the life, and steadied my nerves a little.

Len waited.

Then, in a very low voice, he said, 'Rawle?'

'Don't ever – don't *ever* – let him ... y'know.'

'Like he has you?'

'Yeah.' I nodded. 'You don't know the half, mate.'

'The safe? You asked him?'

'Yeah. A deed box.'

'And?'

'That's all.' I lifted my head, looked into his eyes, and pleaded, 'Don't push it, Len. As a favour ... don't push it. A deed box. That's all.'

He wanted to. I could see it in his face. A thousand questions, and he yearned for a thousand answers ... and, more than that, he *deserved* the answers. But he didn't ask the questions. Not one.

Instead, he said, 'If you're up to it, I'd like to see the place.'

'Me, too ... again.'   I forced myself to be business-like. To shove images to one side; deep-freeze images; meat-hook images.

'If you're up to it,' he said.

'I'll be okay.' I drained the brandy-laced tea.

'Y'know the way?' he asked.

69

'I think so. They did some ducking around, but I know the district. We'll find the shop.'

'My van ... eh? Leave your car parked where it is.'

'Uhuh.' I nodded.

'Then, you can watch for the streets, while I drive.'

He was a lousy liar, but a sweet friend. He didn't know what the hell was bugging me, but he knew I wasn't safe behind a wheel. That's how buddies don't hurt each other's feelings.

You know The Smoke, you don't get lost too easily, so the place didn't take much finding. We made for Chingford, then did a zig-zag route towards Woodford and, in no time at all, we hit the parade of shops. We parked the van, walked along, turned left into the offstreet, then dawdled.

'Not much to look at, from outside,' observed Len.

'Nor from inside ... until you reach the basement.'

We stopped outside a newsagent's, almost opposite the jeweller's; one of those dingy newsagents where they display soft porn all over the window-shelves. So-o – we were two dirty old men, ogling glossy tits and thighs ... the hell we were! We were using the window as a makeshift mirror; weighing the odds and working out the schemes.

Len said, 'He lives over the shop.'

I nodded at a redhead who must have risked double-hernia to contort herself until she was smiling coyly down her own spine at her own arse.

'Back to the cellar-job,' sighed Len.

'I guess.'

That was when I raised my eyes, and spotted the notice. It was in an upper window of the Victorian office-unit conversion, next door to the target shop. I glanced over my shoulder, to double-check. It was there, all right. A few words, some of which were arranged to form the name of a firm, and its address. But the words which interested me filled the middle of the notice.

I returned my attention to the porn window, and my voice was a little breathless, as I said, 'Fingers crossed, Len. I think we've hit a gusher.'

'Where? How?'

'Next to the shop. Top floor. There's a notice in the window.'

He zoomed in on it, and his lips rounded into a silent whistle of delight.

'There has to be a basement,' I said.

'And right next to *our* basement.'

I mentally checked the layout of the jeweller's shop, then moved my head in a tiny nod, and murmured, 'By my reckoning.'

We turned and strolled back towards the main street.

'Lucky,' said Len, softly. Happily.

'We need a little,' I said, with feeling.

Three, maybe four, sauntering steps, then Len said, 'How many people?'

'If we rent that place, we need some sort of front.'

'People in the know?'

'I vote against.'

'Office equipment – we can rent it – a couple of typists ... that's about all.'

'What the hell are they going to type?'

'I dunno.' He grinned. 'What sort of firm are we?'

'Property?'

'Could be. We don't want callers. No reps.'

'Property, then?'

He said, 'Okay. We're a property firm ... with two typists.'

'What the hell do they *type*?' I repeated.

'Christ knows.' The happy grin came, again. 'What *do* they type in those offices?'

We made it to the main street, before I said, 'Len, it's not going to be as easy as that. The front ... they have to know.'

He pondered the remark, until we reached the van then, as he climbed behind the wheel, he said, 'Okay, they have to know.' He paused, then added, 'Anne ... keep it in the family. Just *one* typist?'

'Anne?' The thought startled me.

'She – er – she *knows* ... about you, I mean? About us?'

'Yeah,' I said, slowly.

'She gets a cut, naturally.' He switched the ignition, flipped the gear-stick and moved into the late-afternoon traffic. 'Don't get me wrong, Andy. Whoever's in, gets a split ... family, or whatever.'

I said, 'I'll ask. I'll let you know.'

'Great. I'll work the other end ... fix up to rent the place.'

'You'll need working capital,' I reminded him.

'I have enough ... I think.'

'I'll fix things with Rawle,' I said, grimly. 'It's his bloody deed box ... he can cover the overheads.'

We drove in silence; each working the various angles; each searching for possible snags.

Somewhere near Tower Hamlets I said, 'Property valuers.'

'Eh?'

'It's nice and vague,' I explained. 'Nothing about what *sort* of property. Just so-and-so "Property Valuers". Keep it short, with room to duck ... just in case we get customers.'

'That,' chuckled Len, 'would be a big laugh.'

I nodded, and said, 'Yeah,' but I felt a million miles away from laughing.

ELEVEN...

By the time I reached Putney it was dark. A new night, and a very miserable night; a moon, which couldn't decide whether or not it was fully grown, playing peekaboo from behind scudding clouds, and rain which wasn't *real* rain ... more like a fine spray, trying to lose itself in a cold wind. One of those sort of nights.

The house was unlit, and empty. My darling daughter was away someplace painting the town with her latest batch of playmates.

I garaged the car, then walked through the house, switching on every damn light in the place. I needed light. Light! More light than I could get. More light than I could ever hope for.

Ever played that screwy parlour game? Somebody says, 'Okay, for ten seconds, nobody – *nobody* thinks of an elephant.' Ever play it? It's crazy. That's the only damn thing you *can* think of ... everybody concentrates on elephants.

I was playing that game, solo. But it wasn't elephants. It was warehouses. Fridges. Deep-freezers. You can't control the mind, friend. To tell it not to think of a thing means it's *going* to think of that thing ... that thing, and nothing else. Some of the kook religious boys wouldn't agree; they claim to be able to empty their minds, as easily as you, or I, could empty a tank of water. They end up with nothing – which they call 'peace' ... and maybe they can, and maybe they can't. Hogwash? ... I wouldn't know. But, sure as hell *I* can't pull that trick. Nor could I pull it that evening.

I tried the stereo, but all I got was background music to the same damn thoughts. I tried the box, but it was like watching the printing in a book, but not reading the words.

73

Warehouses.

Fridges.

Deep-freezers.

Holy cow! I was going round the bend. I couldn't even handle my own brain. A bloody fixation. Three things – that's all it could grab ... and, having grabbed, it couldn't let go. A trio. The Holy Trinity. No! ... The *Un*holy Trinity. Glory be to the Warehouse, and to the Fridge, and to the Walk-in Deep-Freeze ... but, after *that*.

That fourth ... 'thing'.

My mind baulked at putting a name to it. It wasn't Muriel. Dead, or alive, it wasn't Muriel. It wasn't even her body – it wasn't *anybody's* body ... it was meat. That's all. Meat, in cold storage.

But, meat that had once been...

'Damn you, Rawle. Damn you to everlasting hell, for what you've done. For what you're capable of. For what you've *shown* me.'

I spoke the words, aloud. In little more than a hoarse whisper ... but aloud, nevertheless. They needed speaking. They required a voice upon which to escape and, with them, came a solemn oath.

Rawle would get back what he'd given. Ounce for ounce. Agony for agony. He wasn't the only man in the world capable of utter bastardy ... and he'd find *that* out, too.

I slopped whisky into a glass, and the neck of the bottle rattled, gently, against the rim of the glass. A triple whisky – at least a triple ... and I downed it at one swallow, then poured more.

I picked up the phone, misdialled, cursed, then dialled again.

Rawle's 'manservant' answered.

'I want Rawle,' I rasped.

'Sorry. He's out.'

'Where?'

'I can't give you ...'

'Get him,' I snarled. 'It's Martin, here. Get the bastard. Tell him I called, and that I want *him* to call *me*.'

'He don't like . . .'

'I don't give one single damn what he likes, or what he dislikes. Get him. Tell him, I want to talk to him about deed-boxes . . . *now!*'

I slammed the receiver back onto its rest.

Rawle was on the line, within ten minutes. He was two things. He was good and mad, and good and worried. He tried to hide his worry, by overacting his anger.

He bawled, 'Martin, I don't like . . .'

'Rawle, I don't like *you*, either. Let's not waste telephone time stating the obvious.'

'You want something?'

'Yeah . . . five grand.'

'You've lost the top of your bloody skull, Martin. You're . . .'

'I'm going to get five G, Rawle. *How* I get it, I don't give a damn . . . but I'm *getting* it.'

'Not from . . .'

'From *you*, bastard. Otherwise that deed-box stays exactly where it is.'

There was a silence then, when he re-started his motor, it had dropped a couple of gears.

In a voice, as cold as the plume of Everest, he said, 'Martin, I could get you dead . . . y'know that?'

'That's one certain way of *not* getting the deed-box.'

'Shurrup about that damn . . .'

'I need five thousand for running expenses. *Then*, I shut up.'

'What the hell's with this "running expenses" routine? What the stinking . . .'

'Cool off, fink.'

'Look, I wanna know . . .'

'Get your bank organised.'

'You think I'm gonna part with . . .'

'Fives, tens and singles. Unmarked.'

'You ain't gonna *get* the damn...'

'At my place. Hammersmith. Your goons know where it is.'

'*I* know where it is. But that don't mean...'

'Tomorrow. After three.'

'*Martin!*' He was damn near choking. 'Just where d'you get all this flash? Just where? Nobody – but *nobody* – uses that talk at me. I been dropping finks like you down deep wells, since before you can remember, sweetie-boy. You forget that ... eh? You start remembering. Fast! For what you just said, I could carve you in little pieces ... and maybe I will, at that. Dream about it, sweetie-boy.'

I gulped whisky while he yapped. I listened to the words, but the words didn't have meaning. When he stopped for breath, I spoke.

I snapped, 'Rawle. Believe me. No dough, no deed-box.'

Then I hung up.

After which ...

How the hell can I explain it? That three – almost four – hours slipped their moorings. It isn't that I forget. It goes deeper than that. There was nothing there *to* forget. A vacuum. A blank. An empty zero. I wasn't alive. I wasn't dead. I wasn't even *around*.

I guess I stayed in the house ... I guess. But that's all it is. A guess. Suppose somebody comes up with the opinion that I took a quick trip to the moon, and back ... I couldn't really *argue*. I couldn't call that opinion pure bullshit – not really ... because I don't *know*.

When I got back – back to the here and now, I mean – it made me think a lot.

Time. Space. But, especially time ... and what the brainbox can do with that particular dimension.

Big moments of years gone ... they seem like only yesterday. Right? For me they do. That, for sure. That first

76

safe I broke; I can remember the maker's name, and the date, on the oval plate fixed to the front; I can even remember the colours of that trade-plate; the tiny scratch-marks around the lock; the paint-daub, along one side of the door; the gloves I wore, the picks I used and that third tumbler ... the one that gave me more trouble than all the others, together. I can remember it, like it was – no, not yesterday – like it was less than an hour ago. Then, the time I triggered the alarm – years later, but still some time back – that was about the third time I worked with Len; not Len's fault – he'd killed everything likely to give us problems – but my fault; a muscle-twitch – that's all – it happens to everybody, at some time; it jerked the probe, and the metal short-circuited the metal of the safe and a wire I shouldn't have gone within inches of; then we both heard the bell – outside – and, for the first few seconds it didn't jell – that it was *us* the alarm was yelling about ... but, when it did jell, did we move!

Years ago. But *not* years ago.

Because, last week ... what the hell happened, this day last week?

Christ knows. That's way back in the mists of time, somewhere. Last week. But the highlights of a lifetime away, they seem 'just now'.

Time don't mean one damn thing and, that evening – after blasting the ears off Rawle – I lost three, maybe four, hours. Hell only knows where they went. I didn't even miss them.

Time clicked into gear again when I heard Anne arrive home. I heard her pause in the hall – presumably, to rid herself of her outdoor clothes – then, she wandered into the room.

She'd been boozing. She was a little drunk, but happy.

She tipped a cheerful wave of hello at me, draped herself

77

into a deep armchair, and said, 'Hiya, pop. Had a lonely night?'

'Lonely,' I agreed, flatly.

'Me? I've been having a ball.'

'I believe.'

'A real swinging ball.'

She fiddled in her handbag. All fingers and thumbs. She eventually pawed out a cigarette case and lighter, and chose a cigarette with all the sombre, clumsy care of a born lush.

This – this was what I'd worked for ... *this*. What I'd spent a fortune on – to give her that stature of 'lady' ... *this*.

She mumbled, 'You ever had grass, pop? Eh? Y'know ... you ever had grass?'

'I have.'

'Y'know what I mean, when I say "grass"?' The question was asked, very solemnly, and with the cigarette held half-way towards her lips.

'I know.'

'Pot. Y'know ... that's what I mean. Good old pot.'

'It's had other names.'

'That a fact?' The cigarette wobbled, away and gone to hell from the flame of the lighter. 'It's had other names ... eh?'

'Viper.'

'What's – er – what's viper?'

'Pot. Grass. You didn't invent the stuff, honey.'

'No – no ... I didn't say that. I didn't say I *invented* grass.'

'Or your generation.'

'No ... I guess not.'

'It's also known as shit.'

'I – didn't know that.'

'A very appropriate name.'

She held the flame to the cigarette, then frowned, and said, 'What – what makes us think these things, pop?'

78

'What things?'

'That – y'know ... that we *do* things?'

She dropped the lighter into her handbag, and took the cigarette from between her lips.

'Different?' I asked.

'Yeah. What makes us think we're *different*?'

'You're not.' I almost smiled.

'Sure ... sure we're not different.'

She took a deep drag on the cigarette and stared across at me, with part-closed, booze-hazed eyes.

'You smoke pot tonight?' I asked.

'Yeah.'

'First time?'

'Very first time, pop. I swear ... very first time.'

'Were you sick?'

'Boy!' She took some smoke into her lungs, then said, 'You have no idea ... no *idea*.'

'I know.'

'I thought I was dying. Y'know ... *dying*.'

'It's not good for you, honey.'

'I thought I was dying. I swear – y'know ... dying.'

'You could get used to it,' I said, sadly.

'You wouldn't mind?'

'Would it matter?'

She lolled back in the chair, smoked her cigarette and watched me with hooded eyes for a while. She was stewed – maybe not quite as stewed as she made believe ... but stewed. Come to that, I'd downed a few during the evening; that, and other things. We made a great pair. If some wise person had blown that house into tiny pieces, at that moment, neither of us could have claimed to be monument material. Maybe we deserved each other ... maybe that, too.

Out of nowhere, she suddenly said, 'I'm a crummy daughter. Right?'

'You're the only one I've got.'

79

'But crummy. Right?'

'I didn't say that.'

'You're a funny guy,' she mused.

'Great. Laugh.'

'No ... I mean that.'

'Yeah. So do I.'

She moved her lips in a slow-motion smile, and said, 'Y'know what?'

'No. Tell me.'

'I think mother really loved you.'

'That's crazy.'

'Still loves you.'

That was even more crazy – it was impossible – but I let it slide past.

'This lover-boy ... Albert,' she slurred.

'Leave it, honey,' I pleaded.

'Dishy. Y'know ... dishy.'

I wrinkled my face into a frown of concentration.

'You *seen* him?' I asked.

'Pictures. Photographs.'

'Oh!'

'She showed me.'

'Photographs?'

'Bathing trunks. Kicking sand in somebody's face, maybe.'

'Over – er – over here?' Dammit I was curious. I wanted to know.

'Sure. When – when he ...' Her voice slurred into silence.

'Honey,' I smiled, 'you're sliced.'

'Yeah ... a little.'

Her eyelids drooped, as the booze squeezed wakefulness out of her. So did her mouth.

I said, 'Mind the cigarette, honey.'

'Eh? Wassat?'

'The cigarette. Screw it out ... okay?'

'Yeah. Okay.' She resurfaced long enough to punch the

cigarette into a stand ashtray, then she said, 'She does ... y'know.'

'What's that?'

'Love you.'

'Sure. Okay,' I said, a little impatiently.

'She – she told me.'

'Yeah ... when she told you I bored the tits off her.'

It was meant to be a crack. Not nasty. A little bitter, perhaps ... but not nasty.

It wasn't nasty. It wasn't even bitter. It was just sour to the taste.

She mumbled, 'I phoned ... this afternoon.'

'You ...' I swallowed, hard, to shift my heart from the back of my throat. Then, I held my jaw tight, and spoke with lip and tongue movement. 'You phoned your mother?'

'Yeah.' She half-opened her eyes, gave a lazy, gassed-out grin and waved a hand. 'Look, pop, don't blow a gasket ... eh? I know the phone bills don't get cheaper, but...'

'No. No. Not that.' I shook my head, jerkily. 'I'm – I'm not worried about the cost. Just that ... You *spoke* to her? In New York?'

'Yeah ... I thought so.'

'Come on, honey. Give!'

'Some dame. It sounded like her. Maybe it *was.*'

'For Christ's sake.'

'Claimed to be Albert's secretary. But – y'know ... I dunno.'

'B-but sounded like Muriel?'

'Yeah. I even called her "mother" ... till she said.'

'In – in New York?' I whispered.

'Some damn secretary.' She sighed. 'Imagine. Pinkerton men have secretaries. How about that? Imagine ... It coulda been mother's voice.'

I breathed, 'Yeah ... imagine.'

'But she ain't arrived. That's what Albert said. Y'know what? ... I don't think she really wants to leave.'

81

'Did – did he say that?'

'Who?'

'Albert. The Albert creep.'

'Naw.' She waved the hand again. '*She* said.'

'Your – your mother?'

'We talked.' There was more hand-waving, more head-rolling, more boozed-up grinning. 'Y'know ... woman-talk. We talked. We said a lot. Y'know ... this and that. And she hinted.'

'You – you actually *talked* to her?'

'Why not? I'm her daughter, ain't I? Why the hell shouldn't I talk to her? Who else ... if not me? Lots of times. We're more like sisters. That's a fact. More like sisters than mother and daughter. People have said that. Lots of people. And, it's a fact. We don't have secrets. We tell each other everything. *Everything.*'

'Today?' I whispered.

'Naw. Not today. I thought so – I was damn sure ... but not today.'

'You're really *sure*?' I croaked.

'Yeah ... I guess. But – y'know ... who knows?' She stared at me with out-of-focus, hang-dog eyes, then muttered, 'Could be. Could be some stupid gag they're working. So, what d'you say, pop?'

'S-say?'

'About having her back?'

I opened and closed my mouth, like a fish taking ant eggs.

'Aw, c'mon, pop,' she pleaded. 'She's allowed one mistake ... eh? Just *one*. She'll be good, from now. I swear. I know her ... she'll be good. Have her back ... eh?'

I wasn't drunk any more. Not even a little drunk. Crazy – out of my head – maybe *that* ... but not drunk.

I managed to choke, 'Yeah,' then eased myself slowly from the chair, and walked out of the room.

* * *

colour ... but, most times, the paint is worn to the same dirty, off-black red. I had to look for the side door; to remember the size of it, the shape of it, the position of the lock ... I had to recognise a whole stinking warehouse, hidden away among Christ knows how many other warehouses, by means of one side door.

It took some finding ... but, after more than an hour, I found it.

From then on, it was easy ... except that it was damn near impossible.

The picklocks played sweet tag with the lock, and the door was mine, within two minutes. The lock was nothing ... but the *door*! All I had to do was open that door, and start walking – start climbing stairs – and, in no time at all, I'd know. What the hell *would* I know?

Somebody, under my skull, was screaming at me to move out. To turn, and run. Not to look – not to make sure ... not to *look*.

I stood there, and argued with the guy inside my skull. I argued with him, and shouted him down, but it took me all of five minutes and, by the time I'd quietened him, I was sweating.

I opened the door, and went into the warehouse.

I closed the door, and started walking. One step at a time, and each step a deliberate effort of will-power. The beam from the pencil torch lost itself in the black emptiness. I heard rats scuffling and pat-patting along, just outside the beam. Warehouse rats; wise old rats who lived fat on the takings of food from all over the world; cunning old rats, who'd sniffed all the poisons and by-passed all the traps; who'd out-witted the terriers and lived to scorn mere cats. My mind played nightmare tricks. The rats were watching me; they were crowding beyond the beam of the torch; an army of rats – battalions of rats – converging, wheeling, forming pincer movements ... waiting, tiny-eyed and eager, until I was too far from the door to reach safety, before they flew at me and dragged me onto the dust-thick floor plankings.

I stood for a moment.

I took a few deep breaths, then growled, 'Don't be a damn fool, Martin. Don't be a damn *fool*.'

It happens. Terror can grip you that way. Tightly enough to make you talk ... to yourself. Like whistling in the dark. Like a kid, singing some dirty song, to show he's a man, as he walks along an unlit passage.

And, no matter how old you are – no matter how tough you are – when you're scared enough, it still becomes neces-sary ... and, it sometimes works.

It worked.

I moved forward again and, this time, I didn't worry too much about the rats. They were still there – I could still hear, but not see, them – but they didn't worry me ... at least, not much.

I climbed the stairs – both sets of stairs – and found my way to the walk-in deep-freeze. I'd found it. Okay – maybe I hadn't really *wanted* to find it ... but I'd found it and, now, all I wanted to do was run.

Run like hell ... then forget it.

Some bloody hope!

I gave myself time to quieten; time for my hands to rid themselves of the shakes. Time to push the foolishness aside, and become what I was ... a pro.

I held the pencil-torch in my mouth, cigar-like. I used the picks and probes on the lock – a good lock – a double-throw, five-lever lock ... and the concentration required to tease the bolt stump through the various gatings held my mind away from other things. I even managed a quick grin of triumph as I felt the bolt ease itself clear of the striking plate.

I returned the picks to their case, and zipped the case shut.

I slammed open the bar-handled latches, top and bottom.

I took the pencil-torch from my mouth, sought the light switch, and flicked it on. A razor fine chink of light rectangled the unlatched door. I doused the pencil-torch, and slipped it into my pocket, then I took a deep breath and swung open the door of the deep-freeze.

Would you believe that what I saw scared me more than what I'd expected to see? I swear ... it gave me the shakes.

Nothing!

Not so much as a chop. Not a single hook. Not even ice ... the refrigeration had been turned off, and the walls ran wet with moisture.

I breathed, 'Sweet Jesus ... what next?'

I was in the right place – the right warehouse – the right freezer ... but *nothing*.

It was like – you know *what* it was like? ... it was like stopping a hearse, half-way through a funeral, taking a peek inside the coffin and finding the body missing.

As goose-pimply as *that*!

Okay ... so it's obvious. Rawle was a very smart boy; he trusted nobody, and he took no risks whatever. So-o, having scared the hell out of me by showing me the freezer, and what the freezer held, he'd emptied the freezer ... on over-drive!

Even I worked that out. Eventually.

But, let me assure you, when you're in an empty ware-house, in the small hours – when you can hear rats doing a follow-your-leader Conga in the darkness – when the last time a door was opened it revealed something Dracula might have thought up, in one of his more nasty moods ... when those are the surrounding circumstances, you don't do much 'working out'. Your brain solidifies. You become scared ... and I *do* mean scared.

I ran all the way back to the Volvo.

Which, in turn, brings up the question.

Why the hell did I go to the warehouse, in the first place? What the hell did I expect? What the hell was I *looking* for?

You ask *me* ... I don't really know.

Except that my dumb, but darling, daughter had hinted that she'd talked over the phone to a person I knew damn well was a corpse. That, after the number of times I'd slammed the knife home – after all that gore-spilling – Muriel had to be dead. She *had* to be!

But – y'know ... maybe there was a seed of doubt. Just a tiny, near-invisible seed.

I think that almost non-existent doubt sent me ... that, and an equally near-non-existent hope.

TWELVE...

I slept late, and awoke with a head like a trip-hammer and a mouth like a camel's shithouse. Compared with the way *I* felt, had I felt merely lousy, I'd have walked the four-minute mile without even being breathless.

I groped my way downstairs, made black coffee thick enough to float concrete, and tried to pour life down my throat.

Anne joined me, in the kitchen. She, too, was in dressing-gown and night-clothes. She, too, looked like something an over-enthusiastic grave-digger had disturbed.

She helped herself to coffee, pulled wry faces as she forced it down, then said, 'Brother! Never again.'

I hadn't the energy to answer stupid questions.

She said, 'You were out, when I went to bed.'

I nodded ... and almost yelled as the trip-hammer did a double-take.

'Where?' she asked.

'Around.'

'Looking for mother.'

'Eh?' I slopped coffee down the front of my dressing-gown.

'You won't find her. Nobody knows.'

'W-w-what?'

'Where she is. I've asked around.'

'Oh!'

'Just that she hasn't gone to America.'

'She – er – she hasn't?'

'Albert would have let me know. We're both getting worried.'

'I'm not,' I muttered. 'I'm – er – I'm not interested.'

'Liar.'

I ran my fingers through my hair, and said, 'Okay, I'm a liar. Let's change the subject.'

'Fine.' She managed a very wan smile. 'What do we talk about?'

The dinosaur-sized question. I knew what I *wanted* to talk about, but that was the one subject I daren't talk about; the subject that brought on a muck-sweat; the big, but forbidden, subject. Muriel. I knew she was dead – long-dead ... long past the stiffening stage. Damn it, I *knew*. I'd killed her. She'd taunted me about the Albert fink, and the shell of 'respectability' had cracked wide open; I'd reverted to my real self – the loner who fights to keep what he owns – and all the regrets in the world couldn't do a resur-rection job.

I filled my mouth with coffee, to give myself thinking space, then I worked out ways of asking. It needed careful handling ... so, I picked my words, one at a time. Gingerly. A little slowly. Saying a little, but meaning a lot.

'I'm a free agent, again,' I remarked.

'Unless you take mother back. Then, if ...'

'I thought we'd explored those possibilities,' I said, grittily.

'Sorry.'

'I'm not an old man.'

89

'No-o ... middle-aged, perhaps.'

'Matured.'

'Okay. I'll buy "matured". What's the big sell?'

'Running a casino can become boring ... even *that* can get boring.'

'As I recall ...'

'Yeah. I know. You told me.'

'A glorified nine–five job.'

'You – er – said.'

'It's what drove mother up the wall.'

'And into the arms of Albert.'

'I thought you said ...'

'I did,' I cut in, hurriedly. 'Let's leave her out of it.'

'Okay.' She lighted the first cigarette of the day. 'What now?'

'Now?' I frowned make-believe surprise.

'Not a rocking-chair, I hope. If you're going to ...'

'No ... no rocking-chair.'

'Still the casinos? A reluctant old age, watching the slobs watching the wheels go round? What a bloody ...'

'No ... not the casinos, either.'

'Ah!' She showed sudden interest.

'I'm – er – looking round,' I hedged.

'For some other sort of work?'

'Naturally.'

'Like what?'

'It's limited.' I reached across and helped myself to a cigarette from the packet she'd left open on the breakfast-bar. She held her lighter for me. Then, I murmured, 'The choice ... it's limited.'

'If you stay straight.' She, too, made it a murmured remark.

'Eh?' I raised mildly surprised eyebrows.

'*If* you stay straight,' she repeated.

I made an 'Mmmm' noise, and waited for the first nibble on the bait.

'You were once unique,' she said, sadly.

'True,' I agreed, softly. Immodestly.

'Pity you've lost the touch.'

I said, 'It can be compared with riding a bicycle.'

'You mean...' She left the sentence unfinished, except for a slow smile of happy understanding.

'I've given it some thought.'

Then, for no damn reason whatever, she snapped, 'In that case, why the hell keep it such a closely guarded secret?'

'Hold it, honey. There's no need to...'

'It's what was driving mother mad.'

I gaped a little.

'Didn't you *know*?'

'Know? Know what?'

'Oh, for God's sake!'

'Okay, honey,' I said, grimly. 'Come off the boil. I'm eager to learn.'

She dragged on her cigarette, then said, 'Look – you glorious idiot – she fell in love with a crook ... right?'

'Right,' I agreed.

'She married a crook ... right?'

'Right, again.'

'Did she ever try to reform you?'

'I didn't need her to...'

'Did she ever *try*? Did she ever complain?'

'No-o. But her father...'

'That sanctimonious prat!'

'You never knew him. He was a good man. He was...'

'He was a pain in the fanny. And mother loathed his guts.'

'Oh!'

'You were everything he *wasn't*.'

'You can say that again.'

'Isn't it getting through to you, yet?' she asked, scornfully.

'If, by that, you mean...'

'I mean she loved you for being what you *were*. That's one of the reasons *why*. And, what did you do? You did an about-face. You became respectable ... *respectable*, for Christ's sake. You, of all people. You were a – a – an aristocrat ... y'know that? An *aristocrat*. And you turned pleb. Like grandfather. Like the one thing she wanted to get away from. Like ...'

'Hold it,' I snarled.

'The hell I'll ...'

'You'll do as you're damn well told, honey. In this house Women's Lib does not prevent you from getting a smack in the mouth if you get *too* bloody stroppy ... even at your age.'

'Okay.' She nodded, slowly and with exaggeration. She pulled hard on her cigarette, then said, 'Okay, big man. I take it you've decided to go bent, again ... right?'

'Did I say that?'

'Yeah ... in Watergate language.'

'Oh!'

'So-o ... do I pass the message?'

'Eh?'

'To mother.'

'Look...' I almost strangled myself in an attempt to get it across to her. I choked, 'Sod "mother". "Mother" saw fit to play toes-up-toes-down with some cheap Yankee wife-chaser. "Mother" can, hereafter, take herself into a quiet corner and go screw herself. Once, and for all, do I make myself clear?'

She smiled, and said, 'Roger ... and out.'

I said, 'Okay. We need a front.'

'We?'

'A front who knows how *not* to ask questions,' I amplified.

'Okay. No more questions.'

'Somebody to sit behind a desk, all day.'

'That should be wildly exciting.'

'Not make smart remarks.'

'A sort of dumb secretary ... right?'

'You'd fit the bill,' I said, bluntly.

'Now you're getting personal,' she sighed.

'Please?' I asked, heavily.

'Yes, father?' She tried her little-girl-perplexed expression for size.

'Do you want the bloody job?'

'Of course. Who else?'

'I wonder,' I mused. 'I just wonder. I only hope I haven't made one more big mistake.'

I didn't hurry the day along. I soaked in the bath a while, then dressed slowly and carefully. Then, I took the Volvo and drove to Fulham, for lunch; to the *Chez Anahid* – one of the lesser, and less expensive eating spots, where they serve duck, in orange sauce, with all the trimmings ... where a man can eat, without hearing the next table's soup-blurpings.

Just before three, I left for Hammersmith, and the casino.

The loot was waiting. Five-thousand leaves of used lettuce, all neatly packed in a wrapped and sealed shoe-box. Five-thousand – don't let 'em kid you, friend ... properly organised, it can fit into surprisingly little space.

Then, on towards Burnt Oak and Len's place. It was Saturday, and the roads weren't too busy. It was a nice, steady drive.

I dumped the shoe-box on the workroom bench, and said, 'Working capital, mate ... with the compliments of Rawle.'

Len gazed at the money, and said, 'How the hell ...'

'I leaned.'

'On *Rawle*?'

'He wants that deed box awful bad.'

93

'Yeah.' Len nodded, slowly. Musingly. 'I wonder.'

'When we open it, we'll know.'

'*Do* we open it?' he asked.

I said, 'With anybody but Rawle, no.'

'But, with Rawle?'

'I have an ambition,' I growled. 'I want to see that particular bastard crawl.'

'Hey, Andy.' Len allowed worry to show itself on his face. 'This vendetta thing ... how come?'

'You suddenly gone pro-Rawle?' I asked gruffly.

'I'm pro that stuff.' He nodded at the shoe-box. 'But, as I recall, this bust was a favour for Rawle ... right?'

I nodded.

He said, 'You don't do favours for people you want to see crawl.'

'I don't trust him.'

'Nor do I.'

'So?'

'He trusts *you* ... five-thousand.'

'That,' I said, 'is an "or else" contribution.'

'And you still hate the man?'

'To put it mildly.'

'Why?'

'It's a personal thing.'

'Not *too* personal, I hope.' He slipped me a very old-fashioned look. 'I mean...'

'Yeah. I know what you mean.'

'It can play hell with calculated risks, Andy.'

'That's what they'll be,' I promised. 'Calculated.'

'It isn't a piggy-bank we're busting.'

'Don't tell *me*. I've been inside.'

'Yeah. Six years ago ... a seven stretch.'

It was a wisecrack. Some people can make wisecracks, and smile, like Len was smiling, and the wisecracks come out very jokey. It's a knack; like being a top grade comedian and insulting an audience. That sort of knack. Len didn't have it ... with Len, and despite the smile, it came out an insult.

In a very hard voice, I said, 'Let's not forget basics, friend. One name from me, and you too could boast a seven stretch.'

'Eh?'

'Just be grateful I don't go for grass ... eh?'

'For Christ's sake, Andy.' He looked shocked, and hurt.

'Forget it,' I grunted.

'Look – you don't think...'

'Forget it. You tried to be funny, and failed. Leave it at that.'

'Hey – look...'

'Leave it at that,' I repeated.

'We ... We...' He shook his head, then frowned and rubbed the nape of his neck. Then he pushed the shoe-box an inch or so along the workbench, and said, 'I – er – I don't think we need this, Andy.'

'What's that supposed to mean?'

'We've never had backing before.'

'That's what he's paying for his damn deed box.'

'No!'

'What the hell else? That's why we're...'

'We're taking whatever else there is.'

'And, if there's nothing?' I asked, harshly.

'A jeweller's?'

'We could be sucked.'

'Andy.' There was pleading in his tone. 'We don't need Rawle's money. Those offices ... I've already contacted the agents. A six-month lease. Starting Monday. It's fixed.'

'You've worked fast.'

'I thought it necessary.'

'Why not give me a ring?' I asked.

'Eh?'

'All this lone-wolf stuff. We work together. We either work together, in all things, or ...'

95

'*For Christ's sake, Andy!*' His temper exploded. Like boiling milk rushing up the side of a pan, it spilled over, before he could control the heat. He snarled, 'I'm the man you need ... remember? I'm the man you came looking for. I didn't *ask*. I was *asked*. By you, mate ... by Andrew Martin. Okay, I agreed. But that doesn't mean I need your permission to visit the bog. It doesn't mean I'm some sort of bloody puppet, and that you pull the bloody strings. Neither you, nor Rawle, mate. I'm – I'm – I'm ...' He worked hard. He turned down the heat, and the milk sank to its normal level. But some had spilled over, and the smell still hung in the air. He muttered, 'I'm sorry. I didn't mean half that stuff.'

He'd meant it.

I didn't blame him. He had more patience than I had; in his shoes I'd have been planting knuckles in teeth, long before he'd lost control.

But, that's a long way from saying I enjoyed being told the truth. It *was* the truth ... but the truth still stank. It stank, but I couldn't sweeten it in any way. I couldn't tell him I'd chopped my wife; that that had been the spring-board – from which had come the visit to Rawle – from which had come the proposition – from which had come my seeking out of Len ... from which had come everything. The knifing of Muriel. The one thing I couldn't tell him but, at the same time, the *reason*.

The truth stank, and that was where the truth started ... but Len couldn't know that.

Ever!

And, a man can only rage against himself for so long. He can scorn himself – be angry with himself – for a very limited period. After that, he has to find some thing – some person – as a receptacle for his fury. Len had happened to be around, at the crucial moment. He'd happened to have made that stupid wisecrack, just when he shouldn't.

Crazy? Life happens to be like that, friend. Half the time

96

it *is* crazy ... and, for much of what remains, it's pure animal.

Len walked past me, and into the shop. I heard him lock and bolt the shop door.

When he returned to the workroom, he said, 'We'll go upstairs, eh? It's more comfortable.'

'Yeah. Fine.'

It hadn't happened. The flare-up ... it hadn't happened. That's what we made believe. But, it *had*, and we both knew it. It had happened, and it could happen again, and we both knew *that*, too. But, we play-acted and, for the moment, we were back on the old two-man-team footing ... almost.

Upstairs was nice; a very homely flat, above the shop.

I figure you can tell a man, by the sort of home he keeps, especially if, like Len, he lives alone. Some are like so many vermin; they eat and sleep in their own muck; beds made about once a month, a sink filled with unwashed crocks and pans, ash-trays overflowing with old cigarette-ends, a permanent tide-mark round the bath – that sort of thing ... a general shambles, coupled with a faint stench of unwashed clothes and B.O. Or, the other kind; the finicky, old-maid type; everything spotless and in its proper place, the brasswork polished, and all the books neatly arranged on the bookshelves, the rugs geometrically positioned and the cushions always fluffed and perfectly placed – their hygiene is such, it's damn near clinical ... and their pad holds as much real comfort as a men's surgical ward in some city hospital.

A few are like Len. Clean, but not too tidy. Their places are both loved and lived-in ... and it shows.

There was a stereo hi-fi in one corner, and some records, still out of their sleeves, on a chair, nearby. There was a modern gas fire, with a neat three-piece suite arranged within comfortable distance. The T.V. didn't dominate the room; it was there, but not *the* most important piece of furniture. Some magazines were stacked in a small pile, at one end of the sofa. There was an inexpensive coffee-table, with beer-mats filched from some nearby bar.

The place had an atmosphere. Cosy. Welcoming. A happy place, with contentment wrapped around it, like a warm eiderdown.

Len waved me into one of the chairs, then bent to turn a control and the gas fire popped into life and added more immediate warmth to the central heating.

'Scotch?' he asked.

'Thanks.'

He opened a cupboard, in a sideboard, took out a partly consumed bottle of *Black and White* and two tumblers. He poured good measure into each tumbler.

'Ice? Water? Soda?' he asked.

'Soda.'

He lifted the siphon from the cupboard, squirted, but didn't drown the whisky.

He carried both glasses to the hearth, handed one to me, then flopped onto the sofa.

He raised his glass, and murmured, 'Here's to.'

'Everything,' I said.

It was good booze, with just the right amount of bite.

We lighted cigarettes, then he leaned back on the sofa, and talked.

He said, 'Those alarms. Let's take them, one at a time. The wall network ... we can assume it's there. Agreed?'

'Agreed,' I grunted. We were moving through his territory, and I was prepared to listen.

He said, 'Okay – wall network. Let's say twenty-six gauge – that's pretty usual – and plastic-covered. Let into the plaster, before the final skimming. Double-pole wiring ... so-o, closed circuit. Those wires are hard drawn, Andy. They snap very easily. And, if they snap ... bingo! That's our first problem. We have to get *at* them, without breaking any of them. It can be done, but it takes a lot of patience.

'Okay – we've had the patience ... we've cleared the wires of plaster, from the outside. We still have to get *through* them. They're never more than six inches apart – up and down, and side to side – and, by my reckoning, we need a yard square hole, for comfort.

'More than that, the hole has to be a yard up, from the floor ... otherwise we're playing pat-ball with the infra-red alarm, inside the vault. I estimate a yard up, should take us above the infra-red beams and, if we eat our way in, about the same distance from the outside wall, what little debris we drop into the vault, before we clear the wires, should fall well clear of the beams.

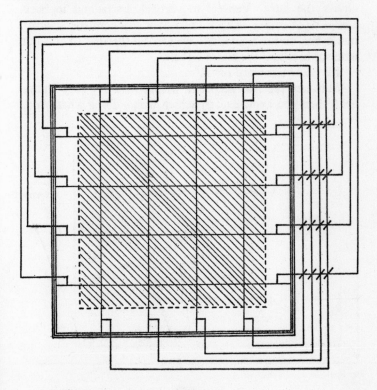

'Okay – that's the problem, as far as the wall network goes. It can be by-passed. It might need a steady hand – steady nerves – to clear the wires of plastic ... but I'm having thoughts along acid lines. Something that'll eat its way through plastic ... then, this.'

'This' was one of two sheets of drawing-paper which, while he'd been talking, he'd slipped from the pages of one of the magazines.

He said, 'I've kept it simple. Four vertical and four horizontal ...'

'Simple?' I murmured.

'... We'll have more than that, of course, but the principle's the same. Vertical to vertical, horizontal to horizontal, spot-solder at each cross-over – where the slanting marks are, on the right – and we can cut the shaded area out without breaking the alarm circuit.'

'I'll take your word for it.'

'Masonry pins, to keep *our* wiring neat ... keep things neat, then you know exactly which wire's doing what. And,

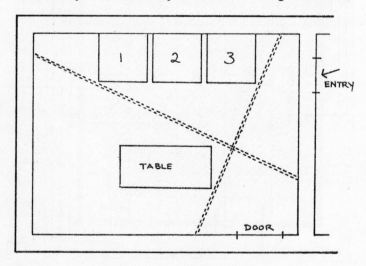

if we can come up with the acid thing, miniature crocodile clips to link our circuit in with theirs.'

'I'll make a few enquiries about the acid,' I promised.

I gazed at the wiring plan. It gradually made sense ... and, like most good schemes, it was simple enough to work.

He handed me the second sheet of drawing paper, and said, 'It's not to scale, of course. But, from the photographs, that's an estimate of where the infra-red beams are.'

'Knee-high?' I said, as I examined the second drawing.

'That's what we estimated.'

'From the photographs.'

'I think we give ourselves enough leeway.'

'And our entry hole's a yard up, from the cellar floor?'

'On our side ... with the hope that the vault floor's the same level.'

'Yeah ... it should be.' I stared at the drawing, then mused, 'So-o, we've one beam to negotiate. Whereas, anybody coming in via the more orthodox way – through the door – would have two beams to clear.'

'Good positioning.'

'*Very* good positioning,' I agreed. 'One beam almost clips a corner of Number One Safe. The other beam almost clips a corner of Number Three Safe. Anybody moving from the safes to the table breaks a beam. From the door to the table, breaks a beam.'

He said, 'We can take a vote on it, if you like, but my advice is don't even touch that table.'

I raised enquiring eyebrows.

He said, 'Concrete floor ... okay, no contact mats. But that table. It's velvet-topped ... right?'

'Right.'

'Where better for a contact mat.'

'Point taken.' I nodded. 'And we don't touch Number One Safe.'

It was his turn to look puzzled.

I said, 'The safe doors. Facing them, they open from left

to right. The door of Number One Safe breaks one of the beams, and, Number Three Safe – we have to be careful ... throw it too far back, and it breaks the other beam. Get it?'

'Anybody being too greedy.' He grinned, ruefully.

'Yeah.'

We mulled the problem for a few silent moments, then he said, 'Under, or over?'

'A plank job.' I didn't hesitate. 'Okay ... let's assume you've got the positions lined up. We check, when we get the wall down. Infra-red goggles. But, even so, a plank job. I want to be *above* those damn beams. I don't want to risk stepping into one, when I have my mind on the safes.'

'Okay,' he agreed, 'a plank job.'

After thirteen years, we were as good as ever. The same dovetailing of minds. The same cool appraisal of the odds. The same feeling of certainty but, at the same time, the same sense of growing excitement.

I've often thought about this feeling. Tried to analyse it.

Other professions carry it, I suppose. The conductor, as he leaves the dressing-room to face some great orchestra. The surgeon, as he makes his way towards the operating theatre. F. S. Trueman, perhaps, when the England skipper tossed him the ball, with the implied instruction to break a pair of particularly annoying batsmen.

And yet, I doubt it – I doubt whether even these men know the full power of this feeling ... music, surgery and cricket not being unlawful professions.

The illegality is the pinch of paprika that makes that subtle difference. The illegality, plus the knowledge, that you're breaking other men's ingenuity and not other men's heads ... that it's brain against brain, not muscle against muscle.

Len was saying, '... that differential air pressure gew-gaw.'

'Er – yeah? ... what about it?' I elbowed the daydreams

aside and dragged myself back to reality.

'It's pretty new.' Len's expression was one of careful concentration. He said, 'I've read about 'em, but we've never tackled one before.'

'The disc, on the wall, above the safes?' I said.

'That's the one. And the fan, in the corner of the ceiling.'

'And?' I asked.

'There's a diaphragm, see?' He used his hands, in an attempt to simplify the explanation. 'Inside that wall-disc, there's a plastic diaphragm. Thin ... thin enough to concave with increased air-pressure. The room's airtight – as near as dammit ... it *has* to be, otherwise the thing wouldn't work. The fan – it's a class fan – expensive ... almost like an air-pump. The fan increases the air-pressure, inside the vault. The pressure works on the diaphragm, and makes it concave. Break the air-seal – make the room less than airtight – and the diaphragm flattens ... and the alarm operates.'

I breathed, 'Christ!'

'I don't know enough about 'em,' he admitted, ruefully. 'Once we're inside the vault, I wouldn't like to risk trying to kill it by messing about with wires.'

'Once we're inside the vault,' I said, 'it'll be too bloody late. Can *you* visualise an airtight room, with a yard-wide hole in its wall?'

'There's a way round it,' he muttered.

'I'm damned if *I* see ...'

'There *has* to be. Some brainy type thought it up. He can be out-thought. Something as simple as planks, to beat the infra-red ... something as simple as *that*. All I have to do is come up with it.'

'Within a week,' I said, gently.

'Eh?'

'A week tomorrow. That's the day. Sunday ... that's Rawle's deadline.'

'Good.' He smiled. 'Saturday and Sunday. Two whole

103

days, Andy. We can beat it – we can beat *anything* – in two uninterrupted days.'

He sounded so damn positive. It was catching. I smiled back at him, and said, 'No sweat, mate. By the way, Anne's the – er – "secretary".'

'You've told her?'

'Yeah.'

'How much?'

'As little as possible . . . and not to ask questions.'

'Great.' The smile expanded into a grin. 'We're moving, mate. We're back in business.'

'I wonder,' I pondered, thoughtfully. 'I wonder what the hell *is* in that deed box.'

THIRTEEN . . .

Think about it . . .

We are not talking about a bloody great bell, stuck on an outside wall. We are not talking about a gramophone record, that plays 'Rule Britannia' along a telephone wire connected to some local nick, every time a gust of wind rattles a not-so-secure door.

These things are ten-a-penny. They are toys. By comparison, they are give-away gimmicks tossed into corn flake packets.

We are talking about micro-switches; contacts on doors . . . and not just a spring-loaded plunger which any amateur can hold back with the blade of a pocket knife. We are talking about a closed circuit, double-pole wire network; a whole room, encased in brittle, plastic-covered netting, hidden under the plasterwork. We are talking about photo-electric cells, and infra-red light beams; expensive gadgets, where the projector lamp needs renewing every five-hundred hours, or so. We are talking about an alarm system geared to air pressure ... *air pressure*, for Christ's sake.

And all this before anybody can get within touching distance of three very fancy safes!

So-o ... for what?

Not for gems. No side-street jeweller handles stones of that weight.

Ergo ... if not for gems, for the deed box.

Think about it ...

I spent the whole of that damn weekend thinking about it. I couldn't sleep for thinking about it. I couldn't relax. I didn't taste my food. It even shifted my thoughts away from Muriel. I couldn't rid my mind of questions. Dozens – scores – *hundreds* of questions.

What the hell was *in* that deed box? Rawle – Rawle, the independent frightener – Rawle, the bastard even the tough babies handled with care ... where the hell did *he* fit into things? Why the five grand? – and why so easily? ... why, when Rawle must have known that any tough talk, on my part, was all bluff? The link, between Rawle and that deed box. The link, between the Jew, Noble, and the deed box. The link, between Rawle and Noble ... and there had to *be* a link. And, if Rawle knew Noble, and Noble knew Rawle, why the hell couldn't Rawle just ask for, or even muscle his way to, that damn deed box?

Questions.

And, from questions sprang more questions. And, from *those* questions, other questions.

I spent the whole of that blasted weekend building a pyramid of questions ... and not even *one* half-hearted answer.

Monday saw some real movement.

Ten o'clock (thereabouts) Len paid in the deposit and collected the keys. He paid by cheque, from an account he'd opened less than thirty minutes before, in a duff name; he wrote, and signed, sloping the letters backwards ... which was not his usual style. What he wore (what he would continue to wear, as a 'property valuer') was not exactly a disguise. No false beards, putty noses – nothing like that – but something to catch the attention, and keep it. An eye-patch. These tricks are as old as the hills, but they still work; short of having time to grow a full set of whiskers, then going clean-shaven after the job, this is the best idea. Something way-out ... unusual enough to stand out, like a red nose on a clown.

The cops were going to ask questions.

And what answers were they going to get? 'He – er – he wore an eye-patch, officer. A black eye-patch. I didn't – y'know ... I didn't notice much else.'

The good old British public. Dumb to the last.

To make doubly-sure, he went 'countrified'. Heavy Harris tweed hacking-jacket, shapeless hat, uncreased Harris tweed trousers and boots big enough to fit a shire-horse. After that, he *couldn't* be from the big city.

We met up at his place, after he'd collected the keys.

My outfit – the one I'd wear, whilever we were 'property valuing' partners – was equally off-putting, as far as personal description was concerned. An equally heavy tweed suit – but without hacking-jacket – and heavy-rimmed, plain-glass specs. I also had a curved meerschaum stuck in my face, and the meerschaum was well-charged with damp tobacco; any prolonged conversation with strangers kept my face well covered, as I wasted matches, and the guy I didn't want to exchange pleasantries with had tobacco smoke blown into his eyes.

These things – small things ... they sort the pro from the part-time.

We drove a hired car to the place we'd rented.

The front door had a Yale lock, but that didn't matter. The front door led into a communal entrance hall, and a key for the lock was included in the bunch.

The whole of the ground floor was taken by a firm of solicitors ... handy, if we needed legal advice in a hurry! The first floor was split, between a typing agency and a flea-bite insurance firm. The second floor – top floor, and our floor – was also split ... some small-time 'general importers' registered office and (but of course!) 'Small and Long, Property Valuers'.

(Hell knows where Len had dredged the idea ... but it wasn't bad. Two pretty ordinary names but, put them together and you get an immediate association of ideas. The association fitted neither Len nor me, and it was one more cloud with which to distract subsequent searchers after descriptions.)

The rooms were crummy, dusty and cobwebbed; at the rent they were asking, we weren't the only criminals around. Two rooms ('inner' and 'outer' offices) and a bog-cum-hand-washing room. There was an old table-desk, a warped filing cabinet and three not-so-steady chairs. There was also a telephone ... disconnected.

'Well?' asked Len.

I held the door, and said, 'First thing, we get a new lock.'

'But, of course.'

'Telephone?'

'Why not?' He grinned. 'Arrange for it to be re-connected, tomorrow. Today, if they will. We won't be in the directory ... and we won't get the bill this side of Sunday.'

'You're not very honest,' I remarked, as I strolled from 'inner' to 'outer'.

'We needn't worry rent-a-desk,' he observed.

'No.' I eyed the furniture. 'A deck-chair, and maybe a card table. That's all she needs.'

'She won't be too comfortable.'

'Great. That should keep her awake.'

'Still ...'

'If she's expecting a penthouse suite, she's in for one hell of a disappointment.'

That was the sort of chit-chat, for about fifteen minutes. Giving the rooms the once-over ... not as 'offices', but as rooms in which we could store equipment prior to the hole-in-the-wall caper.

And, all the time, I kept my leather gloves firmly in position. And, all the time, Len kept his hands tucked neatly away in his trouser pockets. We didn't need to tell each other. We both knew the basics.

As we left, Len said, 'Leave the door to me. I'll have a top grade Ingersol fixed, before the day's out.'

We returned to the ground floor. To the communal entrance hall. We heard typewriters clacking, behind closed doors. We heard voices answering telephones. We saw nobody, and nobody saw us.

Lady Luck was hitching a ride on our shoulders.

In the hall, we turned from the front door, and wandered towards the rear of the building. Along a passage with an unlit bulb, and a passage that (at a guess) never knew what it was like to have the sun's rays touch its walls.

Towards the end of the passage, at the rear of the building, there was a door. It didn't have words on it, and no sound came from the other side.

I glanced at Len, and Len nodded his agreement.

I tried the knob, and the door opened onto concrete stairs leading into the cellars. There was a switch, beyond the door and, when I thumbed it, an unshaded bulb at the bottom of the stairs lighted our way.

I closed the door behind us, and we went exploring.

Some of the doors were locked. Others weren't, and the cellars beyond were storerooms for decaying furniture and cartons stuffed with what looked like old clothes. We moved unhurriedly, and we both kept glancing up at the ceiling ... keeping the topography of the upstairs building in our mind's eye.

We reached the last door on the list – the *important* door – and it was unlocked. There was a light switch, but no bulb, but that didn't matter, I had a pencil torch. It was one more storeroom; more old furniture and cartons ... and, across the room, directly opposite us, another door.

The door.

Len muttered, 'Ten to one, it's nailed up ... or something.'

It wasn't. The hinges were rusty and they squeaked a little, but it opened. Unlike the other doors, it opened towards us.

We soon knew why.

Once upon a time – when 'dear Albert' had been busy figuring out just what *would* amuse his royal missus – this dump had been lived in. The whole shooting-match. Dining-room, library, servants' quarters, butler's pantry ... the lot. And this was the coal cellar.

There wasn't a window, but there was still the bricked-up square where the chute ended. Up above – at street-level – paving-stones covered the place where the circular grate had waited for the heaver to dump in the cobs.

I damn near laughed out loud.

Len breathed, 'Sweet Jesus! It might have been *built* for us.'

And he was so right. We were alongside that vault. It was *there* – only inches away ... and we had as near as dammit to a sound-proof launch pad from which to mount the attack.

We stood there and, for five full minutes, I played the beam of the pencil torch on the coal-scarred brickwork, the ceiling and the concrete floor, which still carried dust particles from the last delivery.

Then, I closed the door and we returned to the hired car.

'I don't like it.'

Len, still with his hands in his pockets, still wearing the eye-patch, leaned back in the front passenger seat of the hired car, rested the nape of his neck against the mock-leather upholstery, and said, 'I don't like it.'

It was the way he said it. The honesty. The deep-down worry.

Ahead of us, a London Passenger Transport twin-decker pulled into the kerb, and I damn near rammed its big, fat, red arse ... then we *would* have had trouble. That's how surprised I was. That's how shocked I was at Len's remark.

I swerved, ignored a blast of pithy Queen's English from an overtaking taxi driver, and said, 'For Christ's sake, Len. What more do you want?'

'I don't want what we've already got,' he said solemnly.

'Eh?'

'We're lucky.'

'So?'

'*Too* lucky ... it'll change, Andy.'

'You would prefer,' I suggested, 'that we have to dig a hole, from the middle of the street, somewhere.'

'You know what I mean.'

'No ... I'm damned if I do.'

'Beginner's Luck. And we're not beginners.'

'We're making a new start – we've been idle for more than ten years ... let's count ourselves as beginners. Does *that* blow away the worry?'

'No,' he sighed.

'Len, don't be stupid,' I growled.

'You know what I mean, mate ... you know what I mean.'

And – yeah – I *did* know what he meant.

Gamblers and crooks. They may not believe in God, they may not believe in fairies, they may not believe in Father Christmas ... but, sure as hell, they believe in luck. And, even *that* isn't strictly true. The only thing they truly believe in is *bad* luck. Good luck, they distrust; they distrust it so utterly, so absolutely, that in time it becomes a form of death wish which they hump around inside their skulls.

My guess is that this comes from caution. Too much caution. Gamblers and crooks – and especially crooks – have been dumped on their respective fannies far too many times ... and for such stupid little reasons.

Take the classic example.

The Big Train bust, and Leatherslade Farm. That farm was a cinch. It was safe – but *safe* ... the mountain-sized police trawl had passed it, and was long gone. All the boys had to do was sit it out, sweat it out, then split the takings. Nobody even *knew*.

Then a dumb dog had to get itself lost. Not even a police dog ... just some canine clown, out for a country stroll and without the sense to know where the hell it was strolling. So-o, it was an Alsatian? There are dumb Alsatians, too.

But, the cops use Alsatians, and some fink panicked. He saw an Alsatian, and jumped to a wrong conclusion ... he figured a flatfoot would come crashing through the under-growth, soon after the dog.

They scattered. They got themselves caught in the mesh.

That's *how* ... and don't let any glory-hunting bogey tell you otherwise. One damn dog, sniffing around for some-where new to piss.

Luck ... get it?

But always *bad* luck. They never trust good luck. They never *believe* good luck. It goes with the rackets. Good luck ... you make your own. Bad luck ... it's always there.

I knew what Len meant. I didn't argue ... not really. Maybe I felt the same way, but wouldn't admit it.

Back at the shop, we parked the car in the yard and dressed ourselves in more civilised clothing.

Len snapped out of his mood a little, sizzled some ham and eggs and, when we were eating, opened up with the beaut of an idea.

He said, 'That air pressure thing. That differential air pressure alarm.'

'Yeah?' I showed interest.

'That coal cellar's made to beat it,' he said.

'Go ahead. I'm listening.'

'An air-lock.' He waved his fork a little, as the idea grabbed and excited him. 'Make the coal cellar air-tight, see? Six-inch-wide strips of adhesive plastic around the door. Around the chute opening, just to be sure. Anywhere where the air might come in. Then, oxygen bottles.'

I asked questions, and he answered them. I thought up snags and, in turn, he worked ways around those snags. That's always the best way. Play at devil's advocacy. Hard. Then, if you're convinced, you're *really* convinced.

I was convinced.

Why not? Len was a good alarm man ... just about the best in the business.

I spent the afternoon driving the hired car.

Surgical gloves from High Wycombe. Surgical tape from Luton. Tilley lamps from Stevenage, and paraffin for them from Hertford. I ordered builder's planks at Hatfield, and trestles at Watford.

A nice, quiet circular tour.

Each time, I parked the car and walked the last few hundred yards. Each time it was necessary, I gave a false name – a different false name each time ... sometimes I wore the specs, sometimes I didn't.

A shopping expedition. Nothing unlawful – nothing illegal either bought, or ordered – but, when we left the vault we'd be leaving many of these things behind. 'Clues' ... if the cops could *make* them 'clues'.

My job was to see they couldn't.

I borrowed (or arranged to borrow) the more exotic paraphernalia, from friends I could trust. The infra-red goggles. Cylinders of oxygen.

I arrived back at the shop, in the early evening.

Len, too, had been busy.

The Ingersol lock was on the door of our 'offices' ... he handed me one of the keys, and I slipped it on my key-ring. He'd hunted around and, at a bookbinding firm, he'd collected a full drum of six-inch-wide adhesive plastic. As a back-up to this plastic – to ensure completely air-tight conditions – he'd purchased a can of modelling wax.

'And this.' He held up a small bottle of faintly discoloured liquid. 'Hydrogen fluoride. Hydrofluoric acid, if you like. It'll need a gutta-percha bottle, before the night's out ... it even eats its way through glass, given time.'

'Hungry,' I murmured.

'It works. I've tried it.' He was like a guru with a new convert; all his previous mood had melted. 'A touch, with a kid's paintbrush, and it *melts*. Then, a splash of water to dilute it ... easy. Bare wire – and wet ... perfect contact.'

'Sounds good.' I tried to share his enthusiasm, but we'd almost switched mood for mood. Now, *I* was the one who had shadowy doubts playing tag with each other at the back of his mind. I forced a grin, and said, 'You're a genius, mate.'

He enthused some more.

He picked up a barometer; an ordinary, buy-one-in-any-instrument-shop barometer, and said, 'These jokers. They work from air-pressure. Get it?'

'Yeah – I know ... but I don't get it.'

'The coal cellar. The air-lock. We take this in, with us. Normal, sea-level pressure, fourteen-point-seven-three pounds per square inch ... right?'

'If you say so.'

'That air pressure gadget, in the vault. It's set for a higher pressure ... must be.'

'I'm with you, so far.'

'So-o ... we open the oxygen cylinders and watch the increasing pressure send the needle climbing. Never mind the "rain", "fine" bits. Concentrate on the numbers. Thirty ... that's the figure to watch. Where it reads "fair". Send it up two – that's a two-inch rise ... one hell of an increase. More than any fan can build, except in strict laboratory conditions. At thirty-two, we're safe. We can knock the hole through into the vault. We'll have a higher pressure in the coal cellar than there is in the vault ... we'll push that bloody gadget even farther from the alarm spot than it normally is. Okay?'

I nodded, and grunted.

I wasn't altogether with him, but I trusted him. When it came to alarm systems, he had a mind like a needle; it found holes nobody else could see, threaded a way through and made everything easy.

He said, 'And water.'

'Why not have water?' I sighed. 'Lots and lots of water.'

I'd already seen it; the plastic container with the trigger-pump action fitted to its screw top. They're for sale at every gardening centre. They're used, by the thousand, for spraying plants with whatever liquid happens to be the 'in' thing with this nation of cabbage-growers.

Len picked it up.

He said, 'That wire network. Think about it, for a minute. It has to be plastered over ... which means, it has to be let into the mix that goes on *before* the plaster. Okay?'

'It follows,' I agreed.

'That mix – about half an inch deep – is at least fifty-per-cent sand. At least fifty-per-cent ... sometimes nearer two-thirds. And it's soft sand.'

'Soft sand?'

'Soft sand,' he repeated. 'Not sharp sand. Sharp sand makes concrete. Soft sand makes plaster ... but it isn't *really* sand.'

'No?'

'No ... it's sandstone, ground fine. It's porous. Very porous. Go to a builder's yard, after a heavy shower. The sharp sand's there, and its damp ... but it's *there*. The soft sand – the ground sandstone – that's soggy and heavy ... and part of it's being washed away by the rain that's already stopped. Brown coloured streams of it, running away from the sand and taking some of the sand with it.'

'Soft sand?' I raised a cynical eyebrow.

'Look, Andy ... that's why they have damp courses. See?'

'If you say so.'

'That's why, if there isn't a damp course, the damp rises and turns the plaster into so much goo ... because of the soft sand.'

'Ah!' My interest was building up a little.

'We're going to hit that plaster, from our side, with water. No chipping. No risking the snapping of those damn wires. We're going to soak that plaster, until we can scrape it clean – ever so gently ... with our fingers, if necessary. Certainly with a knife. And with no pressure at all. We'll *swill* those bloody wires clean of plaster. *Now*, do you get it?'

'Nice,' I said. 'Neat thinking.' And my admiration was quite genuine. Softly – solemnly – I said, 'Y'know, Len ... I'm very glad you're *my* alarm man.'

Then we checked everything; that all the bits and pieces we needed were either there, or organised ... then we toasted the venture in a quick Scotch, and I collected the Volvo, and left for Putney.

That evening ...

I changed my mind, before reaching home. I called at the *Chez Anahid* for a meal. A nice meal, in nice surroundings but, half-way through the meal it hit me ... like an eight-wheeler nudging me in the small of the back.

The age thing. The fact that I'd reached the half-century mark, and that I *felt* like it. I was suddenly very tired; the steam had gone ... all the once-upon-a-time get-up-and-go had got up and gone. People make smart remarks about age, but not when they *feel* it. Then, it is a very unfunny subject.

Could be the afternoon run-around had tired me out a little but – what the hell? – all I'd done was drive a bloody motor car. I hadn't been lifting girders. The hardest worked part of my body had been my arse. So, why the hell was I tired?

Why? ... but I *was*.

Ten years back – twelve years back – I wouldn't have been tired. Tired? On the eve of a bust? Judas Christ, I'd have had springs in my heels. I'd have been itching to eat a way through that wall, and into that vault. Yearning to play puss-in-the-corner with those safes.

Ten years back. Twelve years back.

But, that evening ...

Y'know what I wanted? In all the world – y'know what I wanted? ... the one thing I could never again have? Muriel! I swear. That's what choked me. That Muriel wasn't waiting for me; that the half-sad smile of welcome wasn't mine any more. Wasn't *anybody's*.

I dawdled over the coffee, smoked three cigarettes in a row, and dug deep into caves of consciousness I hadn't previously explored.

Crooks? The bent boys? What the hell sent a man on the twist, in the first place? What the hell turned him rebel? – made him play against a stacked deck knowing that, in time, he had to lose? – knowing that he was trading his freedom? ... for *what*?

Take me ... who else could I use as a yardstick?

My folks were honest. I wasn't the last of a long line of lags. Nothing like that. A sweet and tobacconist's shop – that's where I started ... and, if the old man ever fiddled the books a little, he was never caught, and I never knew about it.

It was said I 'mixed with bad company' – a couple of

probation officers told courts that story, while I was still in my teens – but that was all bananas. I chose my own friends, and the friends I chose were a little noisy and, sometimes, a little rough. Don't get me wrong – we weren't frighteners – we weren't roustabouts – but we didn't take lip and, consequently, we bought ourselves occasional trouble with the law. The old route. Probation, followed by borstal, then graduation to the granite-house itself.

I missed the war – the *real* war ... and I figure that might have had something to do with things. I caught the last few months – between the Berlin bunker and Hiroshima – and, after that, it was all frauleins and under-the-counter sauerkraut. Okay, in its way ... but boring. I enjoyed the spoils of war, without having fought for them. Maybe that had something to do with it.

Out of uniform, I was back in trouble and, in no time at all, I was up in Durham.

H.M. Prison, Durham. Let me tell you ... it was (still is) the 'Eton' of all the horrible places in the U.K. There, you meet the best. You have to *work* to make Durham ... I swear!

And, that's where the bug really sank its teeth deep; where I made the big decision ... to go permanently bent.

This guy I shared a cell with. He was old – older than I am now – but he was a wonder-boy. A marvel. That man! What he didn't know about locks, and safes, you could fit on the sharp end of a needle. And, he was finished – and he knew it – but he was eager to pass the know-how onto a new generation. I represented that generation, and I soaked up the knowledge. Mine was a three stretch – two, with good behaviour and, when I left, I was going to leave him behind ... maybe to end his years in that damn cell.

He taught me, and I learned.

Safes. The square-body safe – the four-bent-corners safe – the twelve-bent-corners safe – the single-unit-body safe ... he drew them, explained them, dated them and itemised

117

their strengths and weakness. The great safe-makers; Chubb – Milner – then Chatwood-Milner. How to rip a safe, how to drill a safe, how to blow a safe, how to pick a safe, how to burn a safe. He knew the tricks, and which tricks would be wasted on which safes.

That old man was a master ... and I was his pupil.

From safes, we moved on to locks. Rim locks, mortise locks, tumbler locks, lever locks, multi-lever locks, pin-tumbler locks, the Bramah-type locks, the detainer locks, the detector locks, the various warded locks – the bullet ward, the collar ward, the sash ward – and, from there to the latches and the dead locks, the single throw locks and the double throw locks, the long throw locks and the hook bolt locks. These – and more – he explained to me; how they worked and how (to the last one) they could be beaten.

I entered Durham jail an all-round yob.

I left Durham jail a potential peterman. I knew all there was to know about the theory ... all I needed was practice and experience.

Just before we shook hands for the last time, the old man warned me. If I ever aimed for the big stuff, I needed a partner; an alarm man. His alarm man had kicked it ... but he had a son and, if rumour was to be believed, the son was even better than the father.

The son? ... Len – who else?

That's how I met Len. That's how we teamed up. And, between us, we'd pulled some beautiful jobs. We were class, and we damn soon became recognised as such ... until eleven years back.

Damn it, we were *still* class!

I sat in the *Chez Anahid*, and worked hard to convince myself of what was nothing less than the truth.

That Len had quietly schlimazelled a way through a triple alarm system. That, once I reached them, I could make those Chubbs sit up and take peanuts. That the loot – and the deed box – were as good as taken.

But...

The kick wasn't there any more. The sweet knowledge that, between us, we could *still* pull the impossible ... it didn't bring on the old glow.

The truth? I was scared. It wasn't the shakes; it wasn't the peculiar brand of stage fright I'd sometimes had in the past; it wasn't butterflies. It was deeper, more basic, than that. It embraced a lot of externals – things that had nothing whatever to do with the break ... Muriel, the cold-blooded contents of a deep-freeze, then the empty deep-freeze, and that bloody deed box. A great mish-mush of unanswerables.

I was scared stupid, and the fear fed upon the fear until I suddenly realised I was panting a little.

Christ!

I paid for the meal, walked around until I found the nearest boozer, then got good and plastered.

FOURTEEN...

I awakened, about dawn, in the bed of some cheap whore.

How the hell I got there ... don't ask *me*. I don't remember the pick-up. I don't even remember her name.

Just that, when I opened my eyes, it was a strange and a not-too-clean bed in a crummy room which stank of old cigarette smoke and penny-a-gallon scent.

I rolled my head on the pillow, saw the not-so-hot face, still wearing smeared lipstick, false eyelashes and patchy face-powder, and I groaned quietly.

She leered back at me, parted the lipstick as a prelude to speech but, before she could say anything, I snarled, 'Shurrup!'

I crawled from between the soiled sheets, made the discovery that I still wore string vest and Y-fronts and located the rest of my clothes draped around various chairs and pouffes.

As I dressed, she asked questions and made remarks.

Sometimes I answered. Sometimes I didn't.

'You were stoned last night, sweetheart . . .'

'Sweetheart, were you stoned . . .'

'You're lucky I happened along, sweetheart . . .'

'Dunno where you'd have ended up, without me, sweetheart.'

'Home,' I growled.

'You're a nice man though, sweetheart . . .'

'A gentleman. Y'know – a real gentleman . . .'

'You had a nice time, sweetheart . . .'

'You had a real nice time, sweetheart . . .'

'I can't remember when *anybody* had such a nice time.'

'You should see a doctor,' I grunted.

'Eh?'

'You're a raving amnesiac.'

'I'm clean, sweetheart . . .'

'Look – honest – I keep myself clean . . .'

'You don't have anything to worry about . . .'

'If you've got something, don't blame me, mac . . .'

'I'm clean. You hear me? I'm clean . . .'

'Look – mister – I don't like those sort of bloody remarks.'

'A favour,' I sighed, as I tied my shoe laces. 'Get out of my life, and keep out. Your name, I don't know. Your name, I don't *want* to know. Nothing! I was pissed out of my mind, last night, and you moved in on me. Sober, I'd have rapped you in the mouth . . . I might even, *yet*. So – as a favour – give your vocal chords a holiday.'

As I shrugged on my coat, she snapped, 'And what about the bread, wise boy?'

'That you should be so lucky!'

She was out of the bed, and at me. She was wearing two

things ... both of them cheap earrings. But her fingers were clawed, and she had long nails. She was good and mad, and she was no lady. The mistake she made was in thinking I was a gentleman.

I didn't wait to be gouged.

I back-handed her, full-beef, right across the kisser ... and she was back on the bed again.

The language was four shades of blue as I straightened my tie, checked that my wallet was still where it should be, and opened the door to go.

As I left, I said, 'Learn by your mistakes, kid. Remember ... just because a man *looks* a sucker, it doesn't always follow.'

I doubt if she heard me. The cuss-words were still on non-repeat when I reached the street.

I collected the Volvo, and drove to a sauna – a *real* sauna, not one of the masturbation parlours – and, having sweated the bad juices out of my system, I breakfasted before going on to Len's place.

Len eyed me, and observed that I looked like something Dracula had dumped with the empties. I let the remark slide past, and we started the day's pantomime.

Having dressed for the parts, we used the hired car, and some empty cartons he'd begged from a nearby store, and did a couple of shuttle-rides to the 'offices' and back. We topped the cartons with innocent-looking ledgers and typing paper but, under the 'innocence' we hid the gear. The gloves and the surgical tape; the wire and the masonry pins; the strip plastic and the modelling wax ... everything, except the oxygen cylinders and the planks and trestles.

I said, 'I'll collect them, tomorrow. Late afternoon. I'll hire a pickup, and deliver after the neighbours have gone home for the day.'

'Back door,' said Len.

'But, of course.'

'I'll be waiting.'

'Sure.'

'One more thing.' He rubbed his jaw, meditatively. 'We do the bust. We come back into the coal cellar.'

'So?' I waited. Something was troubling him ... or, so it seemed.

'When we open the door – the cellar door – we'll break the air-lock. Which means, when we open that door, the differential pressure gadget blows the whistle ... and that's us, with the cops on our tails.'

I began, 'If we're organised ...'

'If we're organised, mate, we *don't* break the air-lock.'

'You're being clever, again,' I said.

'Moderately,' he admitted, modestly.

'Okay ... I'm waiting.'

He grinned, and said, 'Hardboard sheets.'

'And, to you, mate.'

'I spotted some, in one of the other cellars.'

'Okay ... so we don't buy hardboard sheets. Do we *need* 'em?'

The grin stayed, and he said, 'We're back in the cellar ... see? We've just finished the bust. Now – if we hardboard the hole up ... *seal* it, before we open the cellar door. Get it?'

I nodded, slowly, and threw the grin back at him.

He said, 'I estimate about fifteen minutes. No more. But it'll give us a few hours of elbow room. Till somebody goes down to the vault, from the shop.'

'That's well worth fifteen minutes.'

'We've enough tape and wax.'

I stared at him, with exaggerated admiration – but not *too* exaggerated – and said, 'Did I ever mention?'

'What?'

'You're a bloody genius.'

'Yeah ... I've known that for a long time.'

'And modest, with it.'

'Andy,' he said, 'I'll get you there, and back. You make the journey necessary ... that's all.'

'A little side-bet?' I felt very sure of myself.

'What?'

'Ten minutes, for each safe. I've a fiver says I can do it.'

'A fiver on each safe?'

'On each safe.'

'Done.'

That was the mood of that afternoon. Cheerful. Confident. Absolutely sure we'd licked all the problems.

We sat a couple of hours away, in the grimy 'inner office', sipped hot coffee from a Thermos, and planned Tuesday's programme.

Tuesday was going to be the 'making sure' day. The day the amateurs always forget. Tuesday, we'd wear surgical gloves, all day; we'd double-check the equipment; we'd wipe every surface down with meths, to destroy all trace of dabs; we'd check and counter-check, to make damn sure nothing – but *nothing*! – could be traced beyond that building, and used as a lead.

Tuesday was going to be a very busy day.

But, that afternoon – Monday afternoon – we kept the door locked, and talked away the time until we figured respectable 'property valuers' might call it a day.

I drove Len back to the shop, parked the hired car, picked up the Volvo and pointed its nose towards Putney.

Before I went into the house, I bought a copy of that day's *Evening Standard*.

And Rawle was dead – Rawle and the animal he'd called his 'manservant' ... the *Evening Standard* described it as a 'suspected gangland killing'.

I'd made a scratch snack – cheese, crackers and coffee, in the kitchen – prior to running a bath and tarting myself up a little for a mild night on the town. A sort of minicelebration. Like most men, I'd started on the back page – the sports page – and chewed cheese and biscuits as I'd worked my way towards the front ... glancing at the head-lines, and reading the pieces which interested me.

Then, on the front page – a three-column, bottom-corner news item – and the headline SUSPECTED GANG-LAND KILLING. The usual bricks-without-straw write-up. Rawle and his frightener. At the Regent's Park pad. Both bound, hand and foot. Both in a kneeling position. Both shot through the back of the neck.

I breathed, 'Christ!', then went to the phone and dialled Len's number. I dialled it three times, just to be sure. Each time, all I heard was a steady purring ... the 'number unobtainable' tone.

That was when the centipedes started doing ballet steps up and down my spine.

We, of my fraternity, are not like ordinary people. We have a genuine sixth sense; developed, through constant usage, until it is as reliable as sight, hearing, smell or touch. It is a knowledge – a certainty – that the world (*our* world) is about to totter. A knowledge of approaching danger. A certainty of impending disaster.

We *know*!

I drove the Volvo back towards the shop. I drove it faster than the law allows. I took risks – calculated risks – and I was lucky. I didn't hit anything. I didn't nudge another hurrying vehicle ... as I say, I was lucky.

In the glove compartment were the picklocks, the revolver and the spare bullets.

Why? Those who know, will know the answer to that unnecessary question. Because I had this feeling. This knowledge. This certainty.

I parked the car, walked the last few hundred yards and, as I turned a corner, I saw the Capri pull away from the kerb, and drive off. It was among the traffic before I'd time to get the number.

I almost ran the last few yards. Into the shop, through the workroom and up into the living quarters.

No man will ever be more dead.

They'd lashed his wrists and ankles with his own flex; lashed wrists and ankles together, until he was in a kneeling position. He'd toppled sideways, against the front of the sofa, in that position, and the blood soaked the sofa and the carpet, and had splashed chairs and the fire-surround.

Maybe they'd smashed him, before slaughtering him. Maybe they'd hammered his face to pulp. There was no means of knowing. The bullet had gone in at the nape of the neck, and had torn his face away on its way out. It was all around – like gory confetti – tatters of flesh, bits of bone, teeth and splatterdashes of brain tissue.

I murmured, 'They'll pay, mate. That bloody deed box ... whatever it is, they'll pay. They'll scream, before they die, Len. That's a promise.'

It was evening, and it was dusk and, in the gathering gloom of the room, I was talking to carnage ... but Len heard me, and understood.

I was sure of *that*, too.

Len heard me.

FIFTEEN...

7 p.m. ...

I was in the cellars. I was wearing a track-suit and plimsolls, with a woollen skull-cap covering my hair; Len's own gear, which I'd collected, before I'd left the shop. My hands were covered by surgical gloves, with the wrists fixed in position by surgical tape.

I had everything. Two cylinders of oxygen; filched from the rear of a small-time welding firm in the Leytonstone area. Hammers, tile chisels and an unopened box of pencil-torch batteries, taken from Len's place, before I left. All the gear we'd stored upstairs. The picklocks, the Colt and the spare bullets. Clothes and sheets of hardboard, gathered from the other cellars. And, in case I needed it – and I was *going* to need it – an unchristened bottle of whisky.

I did a final, careful check.

Yeah ... I had everything.

I filled and trimmed two Tilley lamps, and then I had real light ... all the light I could wish for.

I uncorked the booze, and enjoyed a quick, nerve-quietening swig.

7.15 p.m. ...

The coal cellar door was becoming air-tight.

I'd taken off the latch, and bunged up the hole with wax. Until I'd learned the gag, the wax had been tricky ... but, heat it a little, over one of the Tilley lamps, then knead it until it feels right, then it's as easy to work as putty.

I'd filled all the cracks, in and around the door, with wax. Now, I was rubbing the plastic strip into position; six-inch-wide strips, with a particularly sticky goo on one side. I went round the door – including the angle at the bottom, between the door and the floor – and I rubbed it hard into place with the heel of my gloved hand. It looked okay, but I made sure; I gave the whole works a second strip, worked hard into the first.

I was sweating a little – panting a little – and it wasn't all due to exertion. That coal cellar *was* air-tight ... and I was using up a lot of air.

The Tilley mantles began to glow a different colour.

It was something I should have guessed, but hadn't. It was nice, though ... to *know*.

I took the valve-key and opened one of the oxygen cylinders.

It was like magic.

Even as I tipped another mouthful of whisky down my throat, the mantles glowed brighter and I breathed easier.

7.30 p.m. ...

That first bloody brick.

Okay, it had to be the most difficult and (okay) it had to be treated with care. It was a nine-inch wall (we'd decided, from the start, that it was a nine-inch wall, which meant no cavity – a cavity would have blown the air-lock gag to hell, and beyond – but cavity walls hadn't been in vogue when they'd built this dump, therefore we'd been as sure as dammit) and, with a nine-incher, it meant that every time I tapped *this* brick the force would be transmitted to the corresponding brick in the vault ... and (maybe) to that fornicating wire mesh inside the plasterwork.

It wasn't a happy feeling.

I stood back, and thought things out.

The plaster had come away, without any problems ... dampness had drained it of all resistance. The same dampness had turned the mortar, between the bricks, into something which (if that bloody wire hadn't been there) would have posed no great problem. But, the brick had to shift and, if it shifted backwards, it could spell kaput to everything.

I decided to try out my new toy.

I fixed the palm-pad onto the drill, chose a bit, pressed the switch and eased the tip into the mortar. It worked! It was like sucking sweets; the mortar spilled out like a miniaturised Niagara. I went all round the brick, two inches deep and, from then on, knew I had the damn thing licked.

Ned's tile chisels were of good, Sheffield steel, and well sharpened and tempered. I'd torn a strip of cloth from one of the old coats I'd brought from one of the other cellars and, with this wound around the head of the hammer, to deaden the sound of metal upon metal, I chipped away at the brick. It was like nibbling it away, crumb at a time but, by slanting the chisel, and not being greedy, it was possible to eat the brick away, without putting direct force onto its fellow in the wall of the vault.

Having chipped two inches, or so, of the brick away, I worked the drill around the mortar again, then started on the rest of the brick.

It was slow work. Patient work. And I'd plenty of time to think.

That (for example) *this* was what top-class thieving boiled down to. The sheer, never-ending patience of craftsmanship; the brand of patience that makes breathtakingly intricate, hand-carved altar screens ... the other side of the same coin. That, given uninterrupted time, there wasn't an alarm system that couldn't be by-passed.

Meanwhile I chipped, and blew brick dust clear of the path I was tap-tapping, towards that blasted vault.

8.30 p.m. ...

After that first brick, it wasn't too difficult.

It wasn't *easy*, because the object of the exercise was to work a way through, and not demolish the whole blasted wall. *I* – not the mortar – had to decide which brick had to come out next; and gently, and one at a time.

Because, all the time, I had to remember that bloody wire mesh. Unseen ... but *there*. Brittle. Ready to snap. *Made* to snap. Invented – manufactured – positioned, in order that it *would* snap, at anything stronger than the slightest touch.

Once or twice, during the past hour – when a brick had wedged, or when some mortar hadn't been as mushy as I'd have liked it to have been – I'd been tempted ... sorely tempted.

Because, you see, I didn't *know*. I wasn't one-hundred-per-cent *sure*. How the hell could I be? How the hell could *anybody* be sure?

I knew about the differential air pressure thing. I knew about the infra-red alarm beams. I knew about *them* – I'd seen them on the photographs ... but that double-pole wire mesh. Who the hell *did* know?

Len had been sure. But, what was 'sure'? A calculated guess ... that's all. Len had given an opinion – no more – that, with the other things, the mesh *had* to be there. But, it had been a guess – that's all ... not a certainty.

So-o, I'd been tempted, once or twice. To risk it *not* being there. To go at the wall bull-headed.

Because – y'see – it had been years since I'd last done a bust. More than a decade. Which meant I was out of practice ... and, by out of practice, I also mean out of mental practice.

And another thing ...

That bloody coal cellar. It was fast assuming the status of unofficial tomb. Claustrophobic. More than a little terrifying. I felt buried alive, and I was scared that the Tilley lamps might fail. Then, darkness – the darkness of a tomb ... and (damn it!) thoughts of Muriel, and a deep-freeze, and ...

I'll be honest. There'd been moments of near-panic.

It wasn't like it *had* been. In the past – with both of us ... when we'd been able to talk. Then, there'd been encouragement and counter-encouragement. And, twin excitements.

Now ...

Holy cow! Now, it was different ... and *awful*.

I gave myself a breather. Smoked a cigarette, took a mouthful of whisky and squatted on the floor, with my back resting against one of the walls. I was filthy, with ancient coal dust, brick dust and general muck. And sweat ... I was sweating like a pig.

I glanced at the barometer. The needle showed thirty-one-point-five ... and climbing. Well past the 'very dry' mark. My ears told me the difference in pressure. They kept popping, then humming ... a faint, near-inaudible hum, as they adjusted to an atmospheric pressure they weren't used to.

I checked the oxygen cylinder. The air was still hissing gently through the valve ... the cylinders weren't going to let me down.

Nevertheless ...

The place was starting to pong a little, and the air wasn't as pleasant to breathe as it might have been.

On an impulse, I turned off one of the Tilley lamps. It might save oxygen – and, if things went wrong, I'd have a spare. Then I moved the one lamp nearer to the brickwork and made a very careful examination of the brickwork of the vault.

We'd been right. It wasn't a cavity wall; it was a simple, nine-inch job ... but. The 'but' concerned a cavity which, strictly speaking, wasn't a cavity. The bricks of the two walls – the wall of the cellar and the wall of the vault – butted up to each other, and there'd be 'locking bricks' spaced around but, brick against brick was one hell of a long way short of an air-tight joint. And it had to be *made* air-tight.

There was only one answer. Enlarge the hole in the cellar wall – make it bigger than the hole I needed in the vault wall – then get cracking again, with modelling wax and strip plastic.

I muttered, 'The flaming thing!' ... but, what else?

I sighed, picked up a tile chisel and the cloth-bound hammer, and started on another brick in the wall of the cellar.

9.45 p.m. ...

I'd been at it for close on three hours, and I was knackered ... well and truly! My hearing was going all to hell and even my sight was starting to be woozy round the edges. The air-pressure was well past the thirty-two mark ... except that not much of the bloody stuff was still air. Half an hour back I'd had a brain-wave. I hauled the oxygen bottle up close to the wall – as near to where I was working as I dare – in the hope that I'd have some sort of relief ... and (okay) in part, it had worked. I was now breathing pure oxygen, plus God only knows what muck, and when things began to get *really* rough I bent closer to the bottle and helped myself to a few lungsful of the un-diluted stuff.

The trouble had been that first bloody brick ... again.

I'd enlarged the hole in the cellar wall, wiped everything as clean as possible, with old rags, torn from the clothes I brought in from the other cellars, then I'd done the modelling-wax–strip-plastic trick.

Then, I'd examined the wrong side of the vault wall, and there'd been this brick ... this fornicating, God-awful brick.

It had looked lousy. Pock-marked. Ready to crumble, at a touch. It had stood out a mile. The obvious one to take out, first.

I kid you not at all.

That bloody brick ... cast-iron would have been softer. More than thirty minutes of nibbling, drilling, sweating and swearing ... and half of the damn thing was still there.

The answer – the *only* answer – was to drill it, hole at a

131

time, into dust. And that was a hair-raising proposition. Because that damn brick was four and a half inches thick, with (at most) half an inch of plaster beyond ... and, somewhere in that plaster was the wire.

The diamond-tipped bit ate its way through brickwork, like a hot knife through butter. There was no real means of knowing *when* ... or *whether*. When it had stopped drilling brick, and was drilling plaster. Whether, if it had moved into the plaster, whether it had snapped one of those bloody wires.

Talk about living on your nerves – talk about piano-strings ... my God!

I'd brought two fire buckets, filled with water, into the cellar. I slopped some of the water onto my filthy, sweat-soaked face, then steadied the drill and prayed.

11 p.m. ...

By Christ ... if ever I needed Len, I needed him then!

The bricks were out. Every last one of the bastards. There, in a heap of muck and rubble, on the floor of the cellar, under the hole. But the rendering – that half-inch or so of plaster-base, separating me from that damn vault – it was cratered with places where the drill had gone just that bit too far.

I wiped the sweat from my face ... and wondered what the hell sort of mess my face was, by that time. Black, and filthy, that for sure.

A bloody good disguise, if I had to run for it ... and (so help me) I didn't *know*. Those wires. Those bloody *wires*.

Four hours. Four hours of donkey work. Four hours of stinking sweat and quivering nerves and, for all I knew, the bogeys were there, waiting for me. Waiting for me to poke a little finger through that last half-inch.

Judas Christ!

I slid down the wall, and stayed in a heap while I got what nerve I still had organised. I slopped water on my face, and tipped booze down my throat, then lighted a cigarette.

And that started the coughing.

I swear ... I thought my lungs were coming up.

That sodding cellar stank like a whore's crotch. Hell alone knew what I'd been breathing for the last few hours ... but, whatever it was, cigarette smoke didn't mix with it too well.

I controlled the coughing and despite its foul taste, finished the cigarette. And, why not? I needed the rest. I deserved it. And, as for lung cancer ... friend, I'd found a much quicker way of killing myself.

I hoisted myself to my feet, picked up the spray bottle, unscrewed its top and filled it with water from one of the buckets.

The first few pumps on the handle – the first water-mist to hit that sandy plaster-base – and I knew Len had come up with another winner.

It came away, like sand-coloured gruel. Like a kid's sand castle hit by an incoming tide. It washed off, slipped down, spilled over the side of the hole and trickled down the wall to soak into the brick rubble.

Within two minutes – before the bottle was half-empty – I could see the red plastic of the wire mesh ... and Len had been so right. It was *there*.

11.20 p.m. ...

Decision time.

The wire was clear. As clean as a whistle, and shining with water in the glare from the Tilley. Beyond the mesh was the back of the plaster itself; a fraction of an inch thin, and all that separated me from the vault.

You see my problem?

Two alarm systems. The mesh and, beyond that film of plaster, the differential air pressure gadget. It was finger-crossing time.

I made the decision.

I checked with the barometer – the needle was bloody near off the dial – then I fixed a new battery into the drill and, carefully (oh, so carefully) guided the bit between the mesh, touched the plaster and pressed the switch.

That's all it needed. One split-second press of the switch ... and I was through. For good measure, I made half a dozen holes.

That was it. Russian Roulette ... the fancy way.

If Len's coal-cellar-air-lock scheme was a winner, I was safe. If not, the bogeys were already on their way. There was no way I could tell, and there wasn't a thing I could do about it.

I took a few deep breaths of whatever it was I'd been breathing for the last few hours, put down the drill and consulted the diagram I'd rescued from the pages of the magazine, on Len's sofa.

One corner of it was stained, where some of his blood touched.

Odd ... it was a little like a scarlet stamp of approval.

11.45 p.m. ...

The wires were about four inches apart; eight verticals and eight horizontals. Which (if I read the diagram right) meant a lot of masonry pins, to keep the by-pass wires in order. Sixteen, slanting out, from the top, right-hand corner of the hole. Eight, slanting out, from the bottom, right-hand corner of the hole. Eight, well away from and slanting out, from the top, left-hand corner. Eight at an angle from the top of the hole – eight at an angle from the bottom of the

hole – eight at an angle from the right side of the hole –
eight at an angle from the left side of the hole ... sixty-four
masonry pins, in all.

I tapped them all into position, very carefully. It was
something to do – something with which to occupy my
mind – pending the possible arrival of the law.

The pins all went in ... and the law didn't show up.

I muttered, 'Bully for you, Len, mate,' and knew that one
alarm had been licked.

Then came the hydrofluoric acid.

I hadn't a kid's paintbrush, but he'd already bottled it in
gutta-percha, and the bottle had a wide neck, so that was
okay. I twisted four strands of by-pass wire together,
wrapped them round with a strip of cloth, then poked them
into the acid.

Then, I touched the mesh, where I wanted bare wire.
Dicey? It was like juggling with cut-throat razors. Twenty-
six gauge and hard drawn ... which is a technical way of
saying that, if a spider took a stroll along one of those wires,
and hiccuped on the way, the wire would go. That's how
gentle I had to be ... but it got done and, by the time I
touched the last wire, the acid was working on the first.

Beautiful ... the plastic ran, like melting sealing-wax.

Midnight ...

The funny bit. The ha-ha episode.

Take me away from locks – take me away from safes –
and I'm dumb, a can-opener is a mechanical wonder, as far
as I'm concerned ... and I had that bloody cat's cradle of
wires to work out.

I'd diluted the acid, by spraying water all over it, and
now all I had to do ...

Brother!

I did it, wire at a time. Checked, double-checked and

triple-checked against the diagram, before I eased the crocodile clips onto the acid-bared wires of the mesh. Like a religious crank going through his genuflections, I wound each wire around its personal masonry pin.

It took a long time ... and, every second of that time, I expected to hear size-tens clumping down the steps and into the vault.

Then, having positioned the wires, I had to use Len's battery-operated iron to spot-solder all the cross-overs.

The funny bit – the ha-ha episode ... Len would have been in stitches if he'd been there to watch.

1 a.m. ...

And I was *in*!

That last bit had added years to my life. The snipping of the mesh, and the gentle easing it out of position. The tapping away of the plaster, until the hole in the plaster was as big as the hole in the brickwork. It had damn near turned me into a nervous wreck.

I tell you...

I hadn't been able to control myself. I'd *had* to scurry to a corner of the coal cellar, lower the trousers of the track-suit and empty my bowels and bladder. I hadn't been able to hold myself – hadn't been able to control the basic functions of my own body.

It gets you that way, sometimes – when things are *really* hairy ... and it didn't add sweetness to the stench in that bloody cellar.

Then (just to make quite sure) I'd opened the valve on the second oxygen bottle, before putting the infra-red goggles into place and easing myself, very gingerly, through the hole.

But, I was there. In the vault. With the three safes in front, and on my right ... beyond one of the alarm beams.

136

With the table in front, and on my left ... beyond both alarm beams. With the door in the corner of the vault, to my left ... again, beyond an alarm beam.

I'd beaten two alarm systems – two extremely *good* alarm systems – and, thanks to the goggles, I could dodge the third.

I checked that I had everything – picklocks, drill and bits, pencil torch – then I lowered myself onto my belly and wormed my way, under the beam, towards the safe.

1.30 a.m. ...

It was easy ... comparatively easy. I knew the locks, and the mechanism of the locks; where the tumblers, and the levers, and the springs were placed. I double-checked, with the feelers and probes, then I set the drill to work. That drill! Those diamond-tipped bits! They sliced room for manoeuvre into the lock mechanisms, duffed the springs to hell, and made the work of the picklocks as easy as kissing apples.

I started on Number Three Safe. It was mine, and I was easing the drawers out and scooping stones and dropping them into my waiting skullcap, within fifteen minutes.

Loot. I was doing mental arithmetic. They were good gems – otherwise, why shove them in a top-grade safe? – and, not counting the gold and silver settings, I estimated the haul from that one safe at around the ten-G mark. I'd worked ... now, it was pay day.

I closed the door of Number Three Safe, and started work on Number Two Safe. The middle safe ... the safe with the deed box.

The drill did an encore. The picklocks did a repeat performance.

And, when I swung the door open, there it was. A deed box. Not as deep as I'd expected – not more than three inches deep – but, by the feel of it, steel, covered with good red leather. It fitted where two drawers should have been. I weighed it, in my hand, and held my ear to it as I shook it. It didn't feel heavy, and nothing rattled.

I emptied the other shelves of stones – just about filling the skullcap – closed the safe door, glanced (a little longingly) at Safe Number One, then slipped the infra-red goggles back into position and crawled my way back to the hole in the wall.

2 a.m. ...

And that was it.

Hardboard, modelling wax and strip plastic covered the hole leading from the cellar to the vault, the stones were stored safely away in a makeshift bag, slung over one shoulder, and I was stripping the plastic from the surround of the cellar door.

I was going to be glad to breath fresh air, again.

I'd left the Tilley burning, to give me light. I'd left the buckets and the cylinders – everything, in fact, except the stones and the deed box – to be collected later, when I'd been up to the 'offices' for a wash-down and a change into my ordinary clothing.

I stripped away the last of the plastic, used a tile chisel to ease the door clear of the modelling wax, then gripped and pulled.

It almost sent me light-headed. The comparatively fresh air, in the cellar beyond the coal cellar. God! For the last few hours I'd had my head in a bloody bog.

I took a deep breath, walked forward a couple of paces ... then froze.

Without even looking, I knew damn well what was poking me in the lower rib.

To make doubly certain, the voice explained the rules of

the game. A very deep voice – as deep, and as vibrant as a double diapason on a first rate church organ – threatening, but cheerful ... as if the owner might break one of your arms, for a practical joke.

The voice said, 'Steady the buffs, Martin. You've done enough work for one night ... you haven't enough energy left to digest bullets.'

SIXTEEN...

The second man said, 'Tell me, Martin. Are the police on their way?'

That's when I recognised him. At first, when he'd strolled into the cellar, thumbed the switch and sent electricity into the bulb they'd screwed into the previously empty holder, I'd had vague stirrings of memory. You know the sort of thing I mean. You see somebody, and your mind says, 'Where have I seen this gink before?' ... that sort of thing.

Then, he spoke and I recognised him.

'Jones!' I said.

'I asked you a question.'

The muzzle dug deeper into my ribs, and I gasped, 'No ... no cops. Not if I've done things right.'

'And, *have* you?'

The question came from the guy with the gun.

I turned to look at him, as I answered, and I almost dropped with shock. I'm no midget – near enough two yards tall, to make no difference – but my eyes came just about level with the zipper which held his leather wind-cheater closed. I raised my eyes. It was a little like going up, in a lift. Flaming red beard, wide, smiling mouth, great hooked nose in a skin the colour of well-tanned leather then – when I was just about getting vertigo – the eyes. Blue eyes ... forget-me-not blue. Happy eyes. Happy *killer's* eyes.

The mouth split into a grin, and showed teeth any horse would have been proud to own.

'Dilton-Emmet,' rumbled the voice.

'Eh?'

'In case you're interested. That's my name. Now – introductions are over – answer the question. Have you done all the right things?'

'I ...' I swallowed, then said, 'I think so.'

'Nice,' murmured the Jones fink.

'Clever,' agreed the yeti-type.

'You – you cops?' I stammered.

'Funny, too.'

As he made the observation, the monster with the shooter reached down and took away my beautiful deed box. Just like that. I unhooked my fingers – fast! ... otherwise, and without much extra effort, he'd have taken my hand with it.

I stared at them, each in turn. They – they *fitted*. Don't ask me what I mean by that ... if you don't know, I can't explain. Just that they *belonged*. Like ham and eggs – fish and chips – roast beef and Yorkshire pudding ... they each needed the other for completion and, together, they were perfect.

The Jones boy. How the hell had I ever been conned into thinking he was a kid? Or scared? *Him* ... scared! That had been some performance because, now, he was being natural and, natural, he looked like he could tame wild tigers, without even spilling ash down his shirt front. The impression was of steel ... and not just any old steel. Toledo steel, fashioned into the finest blade any sword-maker had ever turned out.

And the size-twenty guy. Dilton-Emmet ... Christ, somebody with all that meat *deserved* a double helping of names.

He tossed the deed box across the cellar, Jones caught it, then said, 'That's it, then. Thanks for helping, Martin.'

'Are – are you...' The question had to be asked, even if it killed me, but I hesitated, because it just *might*.

'Yes?' Jones raised a slightly bored eyebrow.

'Did you two kill Rawle?' I breathed.

'No.'

'Len?'

'No.'

'You're – you're not the cops?'

Dilton-Emmet laughed. It was like a force-ten gale, at close quarters, and it damn near lifted me clear of the floor.

Jones murmured, 'Finish the job, Martin. Don't make any mistakes. We'll be in touch.'

I was tired – I was in a state of mild shock – therefore, it took a moment or two for the last bit to percolate.

I blinked, then said, 'Hey – what the hell ...'

It was too late. They'd gone. The Jones guy, I could understand; he was built to move with the speed and silence of a cat. But the big fellow – I mean, that *size* ... and a well-oiled ghost would have made more noise, and moved much slower.

My solemn oath. I glanced down at my empty hand, just to make sure.

They'd *been* ... the deed box was missing.

I breathed, 'Oh, Christ! What next?' and trudged my way towards the stairs.

SEVENTEEN ...

It was starting to be dawn, and I cat-napped a little in the darkened 'office'. I was tired ... the understatement of the century.

I'd shifted all the gear – the cylinders, the lamps, the buckets, the remains of the strip-plastic, modelling wax and wire, *everything* – to beyond the small security of the Ingersol. I'd wiped everything down with paraffin ... as a substitute for meths. I'd cleaned and packed the drill and picklocks. I'd bundled the other gear – the chisels, the hammers, and such like – into a make-do parcel. I'd re-counted the stones, and estimated their worth at around the fifteen-thousand mark ... with the certain knowledge that, because I was in a hurry (and if I was lucky) they might bring one-third of their true value.

However – five-G, tax-free, for one night's work ... it was in the pop-star–bent politician income group.

I thought about it – and other things – as I dozed the time away, waiting for the appropriate o'clock to collect the Volvo and scoot back to Putney.

I could still do it ... that knowledge gave me a nice warm feeling. Despite the passing of time, I could still play footsie with top-grade locks and top-grade safes. I could even by-pass fancy alarm systems ... given the basic know-how. I was good. One of the – probably even *the* – best.

The knowledge gave me a nice warm feeling.

The feeling tended to cool down to zero, however, as the tiredness seeped into my bones.

It wasn't ordinary tiredness. I was honest enough with myself to admit that. Not ordinary tiredness; not tiredness capable of being remedied by sleep. This was a very special brand, and a brand I hadn't tasted before. Before what? Before the Muriel thing ... that's what. A soul-deep weariness, resultant upon squeezing the emotional lemon until there's no juice left ... *that* sort of tiredness.

Thoughts – y'know ... thoughts. Truths, if you like. The sort of truths that bump against the shoreline of consciousness – like flotsam and jetsam of driftwood – when the mind's half asleep.

And, a lot of driftwood flopped around in the shallows,

before it was time to stretch myself fully awake, and leave that office.

They were waiting.

That sixth sense warned me, even before I recognised the car as the Capri. The same sixth sense also told me to keep driving ... and I did. I drove past and, in the mirror, I read the registration number and saw the twin goons sitting up front. They wore their own uniform – wide-brimmed felt hats and trench coats ... gunsel outfits.

The same outfits they'd worn when they'd slaughtered Len.

I *knew* ... that sixth sense told me that, too.

I turned a couple of corners, and parked alongside a telephone kiosk. I dialled nine-nine-nine, asked for the police, gave a phoney name and address, then reported the theft of my car. I gave a good description of the Capri – even the registration number – and added that I'd call in at the cop-house, to make a statement, within the next hour, or so.

After which I went back to the Volvo, did a circuit, parked and watched the Capri, from across the common.

And, let me remind you, friend. It's a fact. Our policemen are wonderful.

The fuzz-cart drove past, braked, then backed up. The blue boys strolled to the Capri, and there was some conversation. Then one of the finks from the Capri was hauled into the squad car, while one of the cops slid behind the wheel of the Capri. I treated myself to a slow grin, as both cars rolled off towards the nearest nick.

With luck the cops would find guns ... maybe even detect a couple of murders.

I started the engine, and headed for home.

EIGHTEEN...

Anne was waiting for me. Up, dressed and overflowing with fire and spit. Jesus! I'd sired a wildcat, and she couldn't wait to get her claws into my hide.

As I walked into the room, she whirled from the window, and spat, 'Well, bastard . . . did you?'

'Eh?'

'You know what I'm talking about, bastard.'

'Back off, honey,' I warned. 'I've had a heavy night.'

'Committing more killing?'

'What the hell . . .'

'Those two men told me. They came to the house a couple of hours ago . . . and they told me.'

I knew which two men, but I asked, nevertheless.

'Which two men?'

'The two the pigs have just picked up.'

'And?'

'They told me. Rawle told *them* . . . *they* told me.'

'Rawle's dead.'

'Rawle told *them*,' she repeated.

Tears spilled from her eyes. Tears of anger – tears of sorrow – tears of frustration . . . I couldn't figure out which. Just tears.

'You believed them?' I asked, hoarsely.

'I'm waiting for you to tell me why I shouldn't believe them.'

'No . . .' I left my mouth open, and shook my head, slowly. I'd had a gutful. I was gagging on my own deep-down misery. I choked, 'No reason. No reason, at all.'

She waited. Tears ran down her cheeks, and she loathed me, but she gave me some small right of audience. I wanted to tell her – to explain – to excuse ... but the words weren't right. No phrase I could conjure up – no diagrams I could draw – would ever make her understand ... and I knew it.

But, I tried.

I said, 'Try to – to...' My voice broke, and I had to swallow, hard, before I made a second try. I muttered, 'Marriage ... I tried. Y'know ... *tried*. Going straight. That's – that's what I thought she'd want. You say – y'know ... you've told me. That that *wasn't* what she wanted. But – but how the hell was I to know? Y'know ... how was *I* to know? I mean, women don't ... It – it isn't usual. Is it? You can't say it's *usual*. Not what they usually want. The – the waiting ... Women want security. Usually.

'So – so why the hell didn't she tell me? Why not tell *me*? Why tell you ... but not me? Just a hint. Y'know ... a hint. Honey – believe me – I screwed myself into the ground, giving her what I thought she wanted. Respectability. Security. The kind of life she wanted ... what I *thought* she wanted.

'It – it wasn't easy. Believe me ... it wasn't easy. But – but for her ... Jesus! I thought it was what she wanted. That's why. The casinos – going straight ... that's *why*. The only reason ... and it took some doing, honey. It took some doing.

'Other women – okay, other women ... I never even looked. You don't have to believe me. It doesn't matter. It's just true ... I never even looked. They were around. The floosies. The tarts. The come-on dames. They were around ... and some good lookers. Younger, too. But – But ... Hellfire, honey, I loved her. That's all. It's that simple. *I loved her*.'

I paused to draw breath – to steel myself for what came next – then I choked, 'So, what did I get? Two-timing ...

that's what. Some bastard called Albert. Some Yankee tom cat, whoring around with *my* wife.

'And, when she told me ... Y'know what? Very "civilised". Out there, in the kitchen ... very "civilised". All the modern, can't-we-still be-friends crap. All *that*. No regrets. Christ, no! No regrets ... she didn't even hint at being sorry. The Albert bastard. He was the cherry on her cake. He was what she'd lived for. Judas Christ – he'd given her nothing ... *nothing*. A steaming prick, maybe ... but that's all. So – can't-we-still-be-friends, and no-hard-feelings talk ... and I was expected to stand there, and nod my head.

'Honey.' My voice became harsh, as the memory sandpapered my nerves raw. 'Honey ... I'm not that *kind*. I don't buy that brand of bullshit. A cross is a cross ... who the hell crosses you. Try to understand that. Try to *understand*. I have honour. That sound stupid, to you? To your generation? Okay – stupid ... but, to me, important. To me, the meaning. To me, the reason for everything. To me, the only thing that matters. Honour – *my* honour ... and she'd crapped on it. That's why. That's a big enough reason why. Again? Okay – I'll not duck the truth ... I'd do it again. Right now. This minute. With all the regrets – with all the heartbreak – with *everything* ... I'd still drive the knife home. I'm that much of an animal, honey, and I can't change. Not that part of me. I still have that brand of pride. I'd *still* drive the knife home.'

And that was it. I'd said it all ... for what difference it was going to make. All! Nothing left. I was empty.

I closed my eyes, and tensed myself for her reply.

I felt her touch me. The nails – the fingers – on my face and feeling for my eyes.

So – okay – I fought back ... what else? That rasping breath from between clenched teeth. Those flailing arms, with the fingers hooked claws, reaching for my flesh. I belted her, then grabbed and held on ... squeezed, and kept on squeezing.

146

How long? Christ knows ... who stop-watches these things?

But (tell me) what else?

What the hell else?

PART TWO

THE SPORT

A large trade in rats is done for sporting purposes at Oxford and Cambridge, where they fetch as much as one shilling each.

RAT

The Harmsworth Encylopaedia

ONE...

There she is. Twisted, boneless and stupid; with her skirt ruffled up, above her thighs, and with one leg of her stocking-tights badly torn at the knee; with one mule missing, and the other hanging to its foot by the toe; with her eyes wide, and her mouth still fighting for a last breath she couldn't suck in.

There she is – twisted, boneless and stupid ... and very dead.

TWO...

Once more, I have a problem. It is a very personal problem. A medical problem – a psychological problem ... *that* sort of problem.

Other people just kill people. People they don't know. People they don't like. Or, maybe, people they don't *dis*like – at least, not too much – for the sake of bread.

Me? I keep it in the family. First my wife, now my daughter. Maybe I should go Abundance, and commit suicide ... maybe I am that brand of nut case.

I decide *not* to go Abundance.

Instead, I decide to be cunning.

I straighten my tie, call in at the bathroom to splash over my face and run a comb through my hair, before taking the stairs back to the Volvo. Then, on towards Burnt Oak – Len's place – with a keen eye watching for fuzz-wagons.

It is no great risk. Len was a very solitary guy; since his wife snuffed her candle, I doubt whether many strangers have visited that upstairs room, where he is now putrefying.

There is, of course, a chance. The Capri goons might have developed a sudden attack of conscience ... but that I doubt. Nobody from *their* university is likely to cough up a killing the cops don't even *know* about. It is also possible that his daughter – or somebody – has telephoned and, receiving no answer, has blown the whistle ... that, too, is possible. But I doubt it.

Nevertheless, I keep my eyes open.

There is nothing. No cars, no cops ... nothing. So, I park the Volvo, stroll into the shop, continue to the work-room and give the shelves a quick going over with my eyes. I keep my hands in my pockets ... because, to do other-wise, after all the recent glove-work would be a little stupid.

What I am looking for is on a shelf, under the bench. Innocently half-hidden, behind a partly-demolished tran-sistor set. The place where a pro hides things. The shoe-box and, inside the shoe-box, five thousand reasons why I needn't be at home, when the cleaning woman calls, later today, and stumbles across a strangled stiff.

I make damn sure I only finger the shoe-box, check that the notes are still there, then walk back to the Volvo.

Poor, dumb Len. He had what he would have called 'principles'. That five-G, for example. He would have starved, rather than touch it. He hadn't 'earned' it ... that's why. It had strings attached or, if not strings, some sort of cockeyed 'charity'. Len? All my life I've been able to read the Lens of this world, like a book. Large print. Cat-sat-on-the-mat language. They'll never cross you, because they figure themselves as honest. I swear. You can meet them on the wrong side of a high wall – doing stretches for jobs they don't even deny ... and they *still* figure themselves as honest.

Good old Len. Good old, reliable Len. Even with you upstairs, staining the carpet with your blood, and the furniture with your brains, you can still be relied upon.

You're still a damn good partner, mate ... and dumb!

Back to the Volvo – back to Putney – then upstairs to pack a suitcase with pyjamas, a toothbrush and a change of socks.

When I get back to the street, the grille of a Merc is sniffing the boot of the Volvo. It is a big Merc. It has to be. It holds a big man ... complete with scarlet whiskers.

Dilton-Emmet waves me towards him and, when I arrive, he treats me to a happy, big-toothed grin, and says, 'You ride with me, Martin.' He jerks his head towards the rear seat of the Merc, and adds, 'Willie Sagar. He'll drive the Volvo.'

'The hell he'll...'

'Or, it stays where it is.'

'Eh?'

'The Volvo. You ride here, with me. The Volvo – it's your car ... make your choice.'

'I – er – ride with you?' I say, slowly. Flatly.

'You've got it.'

'And, if I don't like the arrangement?'

'You *still* ride with me.'

'Just like that?'

He nods his fungus, and keeps right on grinning. I have never seen a man so damn *sure*.

The Willie Sagar character has eased himself out of the Merc. He stands alongside me, and holds out his left hand.

Dilton-Emmet says, 'Give Willie the keys. Don't *always* do things the hard way.'

'Look – what the hell...'

Sagar murmurs, 'Please,' and leans forward a little.

The blade nibbles its way through my clothes and bites into the skin. Just a hair's-breadth, but enough to make me stiffen, and enough to tell me the knife is there. And, this Sagar bastard knows his stuff; he has wedged me neatly between the bodywork of the Merc and the steel of the knife. Short of creeping into the toes of my own shoes, I have no place to hide.

153

'Please,' repeats Sagar, and moves his left hand, invitingly.

As I hand him the keys, I say, 'Drive carefully, buster. That's a good car.'

Sagar takes the keys, and Dilton-Emmet says, 'Sling the suitcase in the back. Ride up front, with me.'

I could argue, I suppose. I could, maybe, scream ... something like that. There are scores of things I could do but, at the moment, I can't think of any.

Except, maybe, one thing.

The cleaning woman books in, in less than an hour, and she is a very conscientious lady ... sometimes, she even comes early!

THREE ...

We have parked the cars in a private, underground park, walked along Newman Street, towards the junction with Eastcastle Street, and climbed three flights of stairs. We are in some sort of office ... 'office', for want of a better word. It does not even *try* to look clean. The words 'K.T. Associates' have once been worked, in gilt paint, on the inside of the window glass, but not much of the 'T' is left, and the gilt of the other lettering is cracked and ready to go. What the hell 'K.T. Associates' are – or were – is not included in the wording. The room has five chairs ... and none of them match. It also has a battered filing cabinet, which is not even closed. It has a grotty table-desk, which no jumble-sale would have as a gift. It has a corner table, upon which are stacked the cheap wherewithall should anybody require tasteless tea, or instant coffee. But, what it has most of is grime ... even the dust has dust.

And yet ...

In my life, I have moved around the shadows, somewhat;

I know all about the world which is not accepted as part of the real world. I am no babe in arms. But, these three boyoes – Jones, Dilton-Emmet and Willie Sagar ... they are the only furniture that *matters*. They are not loud – they are not mouthy – they are not like the ivory-skulled gorillas who shove muscle under an opponent's nose, as the clincher to all arguments. They just *are* ... if you get me. They do not have to prove anything. They are their own proof; that they exist – that you can see them, and hear them ... that is proof enough.

They scare polka dot shit out of me.

Jones is giving out with the 'ifs' and the 'buts'. His voice has a slight, public school drawl ... like a silk glove, drawn tight over brass knuckles.

He is saying, '... Rawle, unfortunately, was ahead of us.'

'Y'mean *that*?'

I nod towards the deed box. The deed box is on the surface of the crummy desk, and the deed box has been opened. Its lock is torn to hell and beyond; no finesse ... the impression is that they have used a mechanical digger to break the damn thing open.

'He knew where it was.' He corrects himself, and says, 'He knew where it was going to *be*. Between certain dates. It's moved around a lot ... until now, we've always been too late.'

'And now, you've caught up with it,' I remark.

'Quite.'

The Willie Sagar guy is leaning with his shoulder blades against the door. At a guess, he is as effective as a bolt, supposing somebody wants to come into this office ... or, conversely, supposing somebody wants to walk *out* of this office. He is not too tall, but he is very wide. Stocky. Thickset. Very muscle-packed, and with that quality of sheer indestructibility which top-class light-heavyweights used to have when Freddie Mills made ring-fighting one of the bloodiest sports ever invented. Not many men have it, these days. Could be Sagar has cornered the market. He speaks little but, what he says rides the broad vowels of the north. He would make a great fighter – indeed, at a guess, he *is* a great fighter – and, with gloves and shorts, he would make a ring the battlefield it was meant to be.

Jones is still drawling.

'Two birds with one stone. We got the papers. We also got you.'

'What am I? The kewpie doll?'

The Alp with the whiskers chuckles, and says, 'No ... the kamikaze.'

This uncle of King Kong – this Dilton-Emmet ogre – is a very happy creature. He is, without doubt, the most cheerful psychopath I have ever encountered. And *big*! ... did I mention his size? He strolls over to the refreshment-making equipment and, as he passes the window, he causes an eclipse; his height and width block out the light ... noticeably.

Jones and I continue the chatter.

He says, 'You stole, of course?'

'Eh?'

'From the safes? Whatever was of value, in the safes ... you took it?'

'Not all of it,' I fence.

'Really?' The raised eyebrow calls me a liar.

'One of the safes, I couldn't open.'

'Ah!'

'Not without breaking an infra-red beam.'

'Oh!' Jones smiles a certain relief. 'Not because you couldn't open the safe?'

'It was a safe.' I move my shoulders.

'So easy?'

I light a cigarette, before answering. I am wandering around in a strange land and, before committing myself further, I wish to examine the terrain.

I blow cigarette smoke, and say, 'You're not cops?'

'Not cops,' agrees Jones.

'Not from one of the mobs?'

'Not criminals.'

Dilton-Emmet adds, 'Not *officially*.'

'So,' I ask, 'who the hell are you?'

'My name's Jones. My colleagues ... Dilton-Emmet and Willie Sagar.'

'And that's supposed to *mean* something?'

'No.' Jones shakes his head.

'So, what the hell ...'

'We don't exist,' drawls Jones.

'Eh?' I stare.

'Officially ... we don't exist.'

Temple bells make warning, tinkling noises, at the back of my brain, and I frown, and say, 'You mean you're government ...'

'We do not even exist, Martin,' says Jones, very slowly. Very deliberately. 'We pick up pieces. We tidy loose ends.'

Sagar growls, 'We do all the dirty work.'

As he plugs in the electric kettle, Dilton-Emmet adds, 'We enjoy ourselves.'

'But,' says Jones, 'we don't exist. Which means, I can't tell you who we are ... because, we *aren't*. Officially, we're all dead ... dead, and cremated. You're talking to ghosts, Martin. Ghosts tell you nothing.'

I glance at Dilton-Emmet, and murmur, '*He's* a ghost? I'd have hated to meet him in a dark alley, when he was alive.'

It amuses the big man. He laughs, and the building seems to shake a little.

'This place.' Jones waves a well-manicured hand. 'It's empty. It's unoccupied. It's not on the market ... but it's been empty, and unused, for years.'

'A place of ghosts,' I say, gently.

'Precisely.' Jones nods, solemnly, then says, 'Now – answer my question ... did you steal from the safes?'

I hesitate, then say, 'Yeah.'

157

'Much?'

'Stones.'

'Their value? An estimate, of course.'

'Fifteen. Thereabouts.'

'Thousand?'

'Market price ... but, they won't be sold on the market.'

'Good. Good.' He nods his head, in solemn approval. 'That's a good enough reason.'

'For what?'

'For the break-in, of course. Noble won't mention the papers to the police. Fifteen thousand ... that's a headline theft, without the deed box.'

'Yeah,' I say. 'What *about* that deed box.'

'Rawle wanted it,' smiles Jones.

'That, I know ... but why?'

'He wasn't alone,' muses Jones. 'Every mobster in the U.K. wanted it. And outside the U.K. The Americans wanted it. And the French, and the Germans. That's why it was always on the move ... one jump ahead of everybody eager to get their hands on it.'

'Okay,' I say. 'Now – suppose you tell *me* ... what's in it?'

'Coded names and addresses.'

'Is that *all*?' I tend to gape a little. Names and addresses – in code ... big deal! I say, 'I could have earned myself a twenty stretch for that damn thing. For names and addresses.'

Sagar grunts, 'You could have got yourself killed, too. Like Rawle. Like half a dozen, before Rawle.'

There is a quiet period. A slice of no-talk. The kettle boils and Dilton-Emmet plays 'mother'; he brews instant coffee in four beakers, sugars and milks it, stirs it, then passes it round.

It tastes lousy ... like sweetened mud.

Jones drops the needle into the groove, again, and talks like he is some professor, holding a one-man seminar, with me at the receiving end.

He says, 'Tell me, Martin. What's peculiar about this day and age?'

I could think of a fancy answer but, somehow, that extra glint in the eyes of Jones discourages any smart talk.

Jones answers the question, himself.

He says, 'Terrorism. It's big business, Martin. It's probably the biggest multi-national of them all. What I'm going to tell you is neither fictional nor confidential. You can get confirmation from any competent journalist in Fleet Street. It's known – it's been hinted at, and more than hinted at ... but the reading public will only believe so much, with their breakfast cereal. Remember the London Airport panic of early 1974? Armed police? The Army covering all the flight-paths?'

I nod. I remember.

'Near-panic.' He smiled a tight, non-humorous smile, and sips at his coffee. 'Not without cause. Four Soviet ground-to-air missiles went missing. Nobody knew where the hell they were. The only thing the Western governments *did* know? ... that they were being passed around, by one terrorist organisation to another. All over Europe. Here, in the U.K. Ground-to-air missiles, for God's sake! Passed, from hand to hand, like so many tubes of Smarties. Inter-terrorist organisation ... that was the first time some of the ostriches dragged their heads from the sand. But, some of us knew – we still know ... we've known for years.'

He sips at the coffee, then continues, 'Think of the better known terror outfits, Martin. The P.L.O. The Baader-Meinhof group. The Japanese Red Army. The I.R.A. The Minutemen. Armies – armies of liberation ... *terrorists*. What the hell they call themselves, that's what they are. Terrorists! And – you have my word – it's big business. It pays good money.

'In 1974, the Arab terrorists, alone, were backed to the tune of one-hundred-and-twenty-million pounds ... in 1974. The governments of the West *know* that. Not guesswork. Knowledge. And, each year, the sum grows. Libya ... forty-million, every year, to the P.L.O. Plus bonuses. An example? A five-million-pound "thank you" for the Munich Olympics massacre. *Facts*, Martin – not rumour ... which makes being a terrorist a very well-paid profession.

'From killing, to protection ... to blackmail. The Black September outfit specialises in all three. So do the Irish crowd ... Catholic and Protestant, alike. Forget religion, Martin. Forget principles. Forget causes. Money – hard cash ... that's the *real* motive-power.

'They work together. The ground-to-air missile thing proved that, beyond doubt. They have territories. Specialist know-how. The Baader-Meinhof crowd go to Jordan for weapon and explosive training. The I.R.A. imported Palestinians to train them in the subtleties of bombing and general terrorism. There's a crowd in South America – they're on the market – anything, anywhere ... except Israelis in Israel. The Japanese Red Army – Holland, France, Israel ... and on "behalf" of the Palestinians. That's how interwoven it is. How close-knit. How tightly organised.'

He leaves a space, and I slip in a question.

I say, 'Noble was a Jew. Full bore. A Yid to his core.'

'So?' Jones looks puzzled.

'You're talking about Arab terrorists. The P.L.O. And – damn it all – documents taken from *Noble*'s safe.'

'Don't be naïve, Martin. Every nation has its traitors. Where safer than in a Jew's vault?'

'Oh!' I hesitate, then say, 'The – er – the Commies?'

'You've still got it all wrong, Martin.' Dilton-Emmet answers my question. 'Ideologies don't come into it ... not at the top end. The mugs – the trigger-boys, the bomb-planters – *they're* fed a load of ideological bullshit ... but that's just to make 'em tick.'

Jones takes up the talk, again, and says, 'Crime ... that's

all. Crime, in a completely new dimension. World crime, carried to its logical conclusion ... that, if you like. It can't be checked by conventional police methods. That's impossible. Two nations – only two – have, so far, accepted the bitter truth. Israel ... their Mossad – their secret police – fights international terrorism, on its own terms. So does Iran. The Shah is a very realistic man – and an absolute monarch ... he's created his own counter-terrorist group. The rest?' Jones shrugs. 'We're democracies, Martin. What the local shopkeeper doesn't wish to believe *isn't*. Not even if his own son gets killed. And, what *isn't* can never be turned into what *is* by a government which, in the long term, sells the people what the people *want* for the sake of future votes.'

Sagar sniffs his disgust, and growls, 'Which is why *we* don't even exist.'

I breathe, 'Christ!'

There is a little more talk along these lines. I listen, in that I hear it, but I don't *really* listen. What I have been told is enough. Jones is no kidder – he doesn't even exaggerate ... I know my fellow-men well enough to spot the lily-gilder at a hundred paces. What Jones has said – what Dilton-Emmet and Sagar have said – is not merely the truth. It is, if anything, less than the truth.

It is a little like being hit across the back of the neck with a brick. No pain, but the same half-stunned feeling. The vague desire to spew. The knowledge that the neck is not a vehicle built to withstand such rough treatment.

Jones is saying, '...therefore, for obvious reasons, Madrid, Cologne and Athens.'

'Eh?' I blink myself back into staggering reality.

'For obvious reasons,' repeats Jones.

'I'm sorry. I wasn't...'

'The triumvirate.'

161

'Which triumvirate?'

'Good God, man, listen.' Jones frowns his annoyance at my lack of attention. 'An ex-Nazi, in Madrid. He was quite safe there, whilever Franco was in power. He's not really *unsafe*, now. A one-time *Union Corse* boss, in Cologne. The necessary link with the drug traffic – the gun-running ... the terrorists concern themselves with these things, as a paying sideline. An English tax-dodger, living in Athens, with influential friends here, in the United Kingdom, and equally influential friends in the Lebanon – in Beirut. Beirut! A hell of a lot of it starts in Beirut. And, of course, with the two main market places for illegal arms deals being London, and Paris, it's...'

'London!' I stare at him.

Dilton-Emmet collects the beakers and, very casually, says, 'Eight million people, Martin. Name the colour, name the creed, name the politics ... they're all here, somewhere. Eight million people – all busy minding their own bloody business ... where else, but London?'

'There are,' says Jones, quietly, 'representatives of every known terrorist organisation here, in London. Living here. Plotting and planning here. The police know. They even know who most of them are ... but, it's a "democracy". Talk. It's *allowed*, Martin. So-o, this is where all the deals are made. This is where all the liaisons are agreed. This is where the information gets passed, from group to group.'

He is standing by the table-desk – alongside the deed box – although, for the life of me, I can't remember seeing him move the two, or three, yards that took him there. He opens the lid, lifts and lets fall back into place typed lists, and documents, which almost fill the box.

He drawls, 'Proof, Martin. Slender proof ... at a guess, half of the people named will be acquitted. But, proof enough to justify raids and arrests.' He closes the deed box, taps the lid with a finger, smiles and goes on, 'The decoding machines have been very busy.'

'You mean...'

'Martin. Grasp the magnitude of the thing, for heaven's sake.' Once more, impatience is injected into his tone. 'It's big. It's world wide. It's intricate. It's involved. Somewhere – *somewhere* – there had to be a key-document. The names, the addresses, the liaisons, the objectives, the arms-dumps, the "safe" routes ... they could all be traced, through this one document. This one *series* of documents. Like the first word of a crossword puzzle. Get it ... and all the other words become possible.'

'There?' I nod at the deed box.

'Rawle knew of its existence. Rawle, and a handful of crooks here, and on the Continent. They had blackmail in mind.' He moves his mouth into a quick, sardonic smile. 'Foolish people ... all of them. Gaddafi, Arafat, the Jihaz al-Rasd outfit – a score of similar organisations – wouldn't have allowed them to live.'

I take a deep breath and stare at that innocuous deed box ... and wonder where the hell that leaves *me*.

Jones says, 'The police are going to be busy, tonight. In the early hours. At least a dozen raids here, in London. More, in the Home Counties. Some in Birmingham, some in Liverpool ... a couple, as far north as Leeds and Newcastle. Our German opposite number is handling the ex-Nazi, in Madrid ... it's only right. The Deuxième Bureau are handling *their* – er – "national", in Cologne. We eliminate the Englishman. I insisted.'

'*We?*' I breathe.

'We four ... having emptied his safe, of course. The next "word" in the crossword puzzle. That's what we're after ... another series of documents.'

'Look!' I object. 'I don't want any part...'

'You know too much,' grunts Sagar.

'And we need an expert, for the safe.'

Dilton-Emmet grins stupid confidence, and rumbles, 'It'll be a jaunt, Martin. Noble in "protective custody", till tomorrow. The coppers are sitting on it, for twenty-four hours ... a simple lock-job, that's all it is, then the balloon can go up.'

I almost plead, 'For God's sake! I'm not...'

'You can handle safes,' snaps Jones.

'Safes? What the hell...'

'We need you. That's enough.'

I simmer a little. Not because I'm here, in this dump of an office. Nor because I've disturbed an unexpected stone, and don't go for the creepy-crawly things which I've inadvertently disturbed. Not for any of these things ... but, because I'm being taken for the complete sucker.

I snarl, 'Jones, you can go straight to hell. One-way ticket. You don't "need" me. On this escapade thing you're cooking up? Me? Judas Christ ... with you three, you need *nobody*. Nitro. T.N.T. Plastic. You're the boom-boom boys. The hero-brigade. I've been around, Jones ... I can recognise the type, every time. Locks? Safes? You'd blow any safe to hell and beyond. And any locks that happen to be in your way. I don't work that angle, Jones, and I'm damned if I'll...'

'Ah, but you *will* ... if necessary.' The big bastard is towering over me. Almost off-handedly, he slips a Luger from the pocket of his wind-cheater, jerks a round into the chamber, thumbs the safety-catch to 'Off', curls a finger through the trigger-guard and rams the snout hard into my gut. He smiles, as he remarks, 'It's the only way you're going to stay perpendicular, old son. We need a safe-man – in a hurry ... because we'd like this to be a polite job, with as little noise as possible. You're nominated, Martin. Proposed, seconded and carried unanimously. You're *in*, boy. Otherwise, you're permanently ... *out*.'

Jones drawls, 'You don't *really* want to die, do you, Martin?'

'What the hell do you think?'

'So-o, you go with us.'

'Up a duck's arse I go with you. You don't need me. And I'm...'

'You're dead, little man.' Dilton-Emmet's eyes are as hard as polished ebony. And as expressionless. Odd – I thought the eyes were blue ... forget-me-not blue. I thought they contained a basic innocence; a foundation of the little-boy-who-never-grew-up syndrome. They are *not* blue ... that, or via some mysterious chemistry of personality, they have darkened. They are the eyes of a killer; merciless, in the true sense of that word ... merciless in that mercy is a quality this man has never known, and never expected.

He murmurs, 'It's the choice you've opted for, Martin.'

'No!'

I can damn near feel the undertaker measuring me for a box. I glance at the other two – at Jones and Sagar – and the fear piles on the pressure until the point of terror is reached. Terror ... caused by the complete lack of interest shown by either Jones or Sagar. Terror ... increased to frantic self-preservation, as I see the big man's finger tighten around the Luger's trigger.

I breath, 'No! For God's sake. I – I don't go for the muscle angle. It's – it's not my thing.'

Jones closes the lid of the deed box. Casually. Without haste.

He purrs, 'You must remember, Martin ... we don't even exist. That being the case, the law doesn't apply.'

I beat the bullet ... just.

'No! I'll do it. Anything! I'll do it.'

The voice is mine. Screaming. I don't recognise it. Never before have I forced such a scream past a tightened throat. Never before have I used such a voice. Never ... and yet the voice is mine.

The miracle happens. An optical illusion, perhaps ... but, to me, a miracle. The eyes take on life – they lose their blackness – they once more become a gentle shade of forget-me-not blue.

He thumbs on the safety-catch, uncocks the Luger, treats me to a friendly smile, and rumbles, 'Of course you will, old son. We need you. That's enough. Whoever thought you wouldn't?'

I nod, dumbly, and try to stop the tremble in my legs.

FOUR...

Let me tell you...

The fireworks are due to start at three o'clock, G.M.T. Three o'clock in the morning. *This* morning. Everything. In the U.K. a lot of nasty bastards, and a lot of not-too-nice dames are due to have their beauty sleep interrupted. The Met bogeys have things tightly organised at their end. A lot of fuzz armies are equally tightly organised elsewhere; a lot of doors are due to be knocked on, and a lot of collars are due to be felt.

Great ... three o'clock.

Three o'clock, G.M.T., also for the lash-ups in Madrid, Cologne and Athens.

A good time is about to be had by all, at three o'clock, G.M.T.

Except...

There are snags, and the biggest snag of all is that I am here, on this highly uncomfortable seat, in this string-bag of an army transport plane, surrounded by a lot of unoccupied seats, Dilton-Emmet and Sagar. The two original death-or-glory boys, and yours truly.

And these two bananas are quietly preparing themselves ... for what? For a sweet state of affairs which, with a modicum of luck, could very easily blow itself up into an 'international incident', complete with gunboats, opposing armies and all the other frills which go to make up the modern war which is never *called* a war? That? I wouldn't know ... I am along strictly for the ride.

Or, am I?

A thought strikes me, and it is not a very comforting thought. That maybe we are spies. Saboteurs. Something fancy, like that. Which could mean some stinking Greek prison, for a long, long time, if not a last cigarette at dawn.

I am too old for this lark ... that, what the hell we are. And I wish I was not one of us. I am an old man. I have greying hair and stiffening joints. I am well past the fighting age, and I have never counted blood as my favourite colour ... especially *my* blood.

Judas Christ, what the hell am I *doing* here?

Jones wanders in, from the pilot's cabin. He looks pleased.

He says, 'The Madrid and Cologne raids are on schedule.'

Sagar grunts, 'Great.'

Great! That's all. That is the only reaction to what could be the start whistle for World War III, for all I know. I swear ... I am in the company of a trio of certifiable nuts.

And, another thing...

Three o'clock in the morning. It is a very appropriate time for catching the opposition with their braces dangling. Right? But, in Athens, it is *not* three o'clock in the morning. In Athens it is *one* o'clock in the morning ... which makes one hell of a difference.

People – especially rich Englishmen, living abroad – keep very uncertain hours. Could be the kink we're after does not retire until well after one o'clock and, whereas some of my fellow lifters like the extra thrill of doing their light-fingered removing while life stirs around in adjoining rooms, I can live *without* that extra thrill. I do not even like other people to be *there*.

I glance at my watch, and worry some more. The berk whose home we are about to rifle could still be arsing around doing a Zorba-the-Greek one-step because, by Athens time, it is not yet midnight.

I turn my head and look out of a port-hole-shaped window.

Nothing ... it is like squinting down the neck of an ink bottle. I recall the o'clock, and try to remember what little I learned in the geography class. By my reckoning, we should be over the Ionian Sea. A very nice sea – so I'm told ... but, still wet. After which comes Morea, complete with Arcadia. And there's a thing. Arcadia. A very gummy place about which to write an operetta ... especially from where I'm sitting. Then, a quick nip across the Gulf of Aegina, and we're there. Athens airport – supposing they are dumb enough to let us land ... and we are a damn sight too close for *my* peace of mind.

This (I tell myself) is what is called 'adventure'. This is the crap with medals attached; the stuff of which movies are made. Red-blooded stuff, to keep the customers on the edge of their seats; the big build-up, before the smash ending.

So-o ... all we need is Burt Lancaster.

But, we don't *have* Burt Lancaster ... and this is for real.

I stroke the case of picklocks, resting on my knee. *They* are real. They are the only tiny piece of reality in this whole inverted Alice-in-Gooneyland into which I have been hustled.

Dilton-Emmet lumbers down the centre of the gangway. He has a Red Devil beret pulled to a piratical angle over his thatch. All he needs is a naked blade between those grinning teeth, and Morgan himself would fight a way out of his grave to stand alongside him. Odd. I suddenly feel a little less scared. Not brave, you understand ... but, just a *leetle* less worried.

'Happy?' he asks, in a friendly growl.

'Yeah ... hilarious.'

'This,' he pronounces, 'is what makes life.'

'Or the other thing.'

'In which case, you've damn-all to worry about.'

'I've heard the gag,' I say, sourly.

'It's a quiet job,' he promises. 'Just to get you to the safe ... that's all.'

'And?'

'No unnecessary rough stuff. Orders.'

I say, 'You? Orders? The two don't dovetail, big man.'

'Everything,' he assures me, with a grin. 'Everything I do.'

I shake my head in disbelief.

'Hey, Martin.' He squats his bulk alongside me. 'No more worries ... right. You're here to crack a safe. That's all. More papers. More names and addresses. You'll do it.'

'Yeah ... I'll do it.'

'So, no more butterflies. Stay between Sagar and me. We've done it all before.'

'That, I believe.'

'We don't die.'

'No?'

'No.' The grin widens. I believe him, when he says, 'We have this philosophy. We make sure the other bastard dies first.'

He takes the Luger from a pocket of his windcheater and, from another pocket he takes a cylindrical silencer. He screws the silencer onto the business-end of the Luger.

'A quiet job,' I murmur, sarcastically.

'This makes it quiet.' He taps the silencer with a fore-finger.

'But, of course.'

'I didn't say no shooting ... did I?'

'No,' I agree, flatly. 'You didn't say no shooting.'

'No *unnecessary* shooting. That's the order.'

'What's "necessary"?' I ask, wearily.

'When the other man has a gun.'

'That easy?'

'That easy,' he agrees.

I believe him, too. This overgrown hit man makes any-thing believable. Anything possible.

169

Nevertheless...

'How the hell,' I ask, 'are you going to get the iron-mongery past the check-point at the terminal?'

'Easy.'

'But, naturally.'

'We don't go through the check-point.'

'Holy cow!'

'The drachma talks as loud as the dollar, son.'

'And, if it suddenly gets tongue-tied? If things go wrong?'

'The usual.' He chuckles. 'A couple of weeks in a cell, to await diplomatic bowings, scrapings and apologies. But things don't go wrong. Not with us.'

'This outfit you're in...'

'Don't ask.' He is suddenly very serious.

'It can get away with anything. That it?'

'It can try. It hasn't failed yet.'

I shake my head in wonderment.

Sagar joins us. He, too, is hefting a silencered Luger.

He says, 'There's a spare shooter, Martin.'

'I don't need one. I'm here to drill holes in metal ... not flesh.'

'Okay. Do it well.'

I nod. I am past speech. This thing – whatever it is – I am up to the eyeballs, whether I like it, or not ... and chances are I'm likely to have my guts blown through my spine, before dawn.

It is not a cosy thought.

FIVE...

Somebody, somewhere, is very hot on organisation.

A Jeep is waiting for us, on the apron, and there is no customs check-out. Sagar, with Jones sitting alongside him, drives the Jeep around the perimeter, and we leave the airport via a rear gate. I share the rear seat with the hairy monster, and some dumb, uniformed official holds the gate open for us, and even salutes, as we pass.

Dilton-Emmet chuckles, and says, 'Drachmas ... didn't I tell you?'

'Such a lot of things,' I agree.

After that, nobody says much ... in this sort of situation, what the hell *is* there to say?

Eight miles, due north-west, we hit the outskirts of Athens.

'The City of the Violet Crown.' That is what the creeps who handle flash language call the place; the 'chief city of Attica in Classical times'. Let me tell you. This is no holiday brochure, so here comes the truth.

We are coming into this very fancy city along a road which flanks the River Ilissos and, from where I am sitting, I can see most things. I have a very good view, and the main landscape consists of the usual geometric garbage common to *all* cities. Skyscrapers, office-blocks, snazzy hotels and high-rise flats ... and a lot of trick electricity.

I have been conned.

According to all the legends I have been force-fed, throughout my youth, and adult life, we should be driving a hole through history. The Rock of Acropolis should be on our left, with the Parthenon on its peak. There should also be the Theatre Herodes and the Theatre of Dionysos around to take my breath away.

Nothing!

I have a fleeting suspicion that some money-grabbing jerk has turned them all into clip-joints without mentioning that small fact to the city fathers.

The Jeep goes straight ahead for a while, then takes a sharp turn right.

Maybe Jones is a thought-reader, because he says, 'The Temple of Zeus.'

I twist my neck, and say, 'Eh? Where?'

'We've just passed it.'

'The hell we have.'

'At the corner.'

'Some bloody temple,' I growl. 'That's the Temple of Zeus ... that was. I thought they went in for size.'

'Beauty,' Jones corrects me.

'Okay – beauty ... but, at least, somebody could have put a sign up.'

Alongside me, Dilton-Emmet chuckles quietly, to himself. He's guessed. He knows. All my empty talk is just that ... empty talk. A counter to the knots into which my guts are busy tying themselves. I talk, because I am many things. Scared, mostly. But, also excited – taut – breathless – as ready for this farrago as I am ever likely to be ... but, mostly, scared.

He murmurs, 'Not long now, boy.'

Jones holds his wrist low, to catch the glow from the dash. I lean forward, to read the face of his watch, with him. It still gives G.M.T. The hands show less than fifteen minutes to 3 a.m.

There is nothing Grecian about *this* place. Beyond the fence, the subdued moonlight shows a two-tier, squat building, surrounded by cypress- and aromatic-shrub-interrupted lawns. They are good lawns. Immaculate *English* lawns. In this part of the globe they are unique lawns, and Christ alone knows how much money it takes to keep them in this condition.

The tar-mac drive, from the locked gates, snakes elegantly through these lawns before encircling the house.

The house itself?

I tell you what it looks like, to *me*. A bloody castle! Nothing less. It carries an air of invincibility; as if it could shrug off an army. It is made of stone and, even from this distance, the walls, the windows and the doors look uncommonly thick and monumentally strong. If the guy we are after is behind those walls, and if I was the guy we are after, I would, at this moment, be quite unworried.

Four of us – correction ... three of *them*, plus little old me as a stand-by spectator. And this trio of lunatics figure we're going to crack *this*.

The Jeep is parked in the shadows of a grove of trees, about a quarter of a mile away. Athens is four – maybe five – miles to our west. Sagar has melted off into the darkness, on his own pre-arranged errand, and Jones, Dilton-Emmet and I are standing here, in the thickest shadows we can find, waiting.

For the last five minutes, or so, I have been staring at a link-wire fence. A strong fence, with steel stanchions every few yards, and a fence which (for my money) encircles the whole of the grounds. The last twelve inches of each stanchion angle outwards, and these angles are linked together by a trio of equidistant copper wires ... and, five gets you five hundred, each of those copper wires carries one hell of a voltage.

Brother ... do I wish we numbered five, and that the fifth was Len!

Len would know. By this time he'd have figured a way to tame those damn copper wires. By this time, they'd be sitting up and taking peanuts. But, not me. Jones and his brace of tame heavies have made a mistake; they don't know the difference between a safe-man and an alarm-man; it hasn't jelled that I kiboshed the vault alarm systems at Noble's place because Len had already shown me *how* to kibosh them ... and drawn plans.

I swallow, to moisten my throat, then whisper, 'Look – those wires, above the fence.'

'Alarm wires,' murmurs Jones.

'Yeah, I know. That's what ...'

'High-voltage, at a guess.'

If it is possible to breathe a groan, that is what I do. I say,

173

'I'm no hot-wire expert, Jones. I wouldn't know how to start.'

'Climb up, and grab one of 'em,' rumbles the big man.

'Wha-at?'

'Then grab a handful of the link-wire.'

'For Christ's sake!'

'If your eyes light up, we'll know there's juice going through 'em.' He chuckles, quietly, and adds. 'Hold your bladder, Martin. We're not going over. We're using the gate.'

'Oh!'

'Quiet.' Jones holds his watch closer to his face. 'Twenty seconds ... where the hell's Sagar?'

'Right here.' Sagar is with us ... he arrived with all the fanfare of a well-trained ghost. He murmurs, 'Okay. They're off the telephone network.'

'Good.' Jones taps the big man's arm. 'On your way, friend. And, good luck.'

And the curtain goes up on the pantomime.

3 a.m. (G.M.T.)...

Dilton-Emmet strolls from cover and makes for the gate. He leans his thumb against a bell-push let into one of the concrete pillars upon which the gates are hung.

There is a gate-house – a one-storey miniature bungalow-like building – and, within a minute, or so, a light is switched on and a lanky, tough-faced hombre opens the door of the gate-house, blinks cat-nap sleep from his eyes and walks to the gate. He is coatless, and his tie is loosened at the collar of his shirt. As he approaches the big man, he settles a holster into position on the belt on his pants.

There is some chit-chat we cannot catch, and the big man holds something out, through the bars of the gate and towards the approaching guard. Could be it is a bank-card –

something like that – it *looks* like a bank-card, from where I crouch ... but, whatever it is, it does the trick. The guard moves in close, lowers his eyes and begins to raise a hand to take the card. The big man moves. And, Christ, the *speed* of his movement. He lets the card slip from his fingers, grabs a fistful of the guard's shirt, yanks and slams the face of the guard onto the steel uprights of the gate.

You have my word. The guard is in Dreamland, before the card reaches the tar-mac of the drive.

Jones snaps, 'In we go,' and he, and Sagar, sprint for the gates.

I follow.

What else? Where else have I to go?

3.03 a.m. (G.M.T.) ...

It is minute by minute stuff ... and every minute stretches itself out, until it takes almost an hour to move into history.

The big man holds the guard upright, while Sagar fishes around, and finds a chain, with a key-ring attached, at the rear of the guard's belt. Sagar starts fitting the keys into the lock, on the inside of the gate.

A dog comes from the gate-house. It is a very nasty-looking dog; a man-mauler; a dobermann pinscher. It takes an immediate dislike to what is going on. It gives out a snarling growl, and launches itself at the big man's wrist and forearm ... but never gets there. Jones, too, has a silencered Luger, and Jones's Luger makes a noise no louder that a handful of putty hitting a stone floor from waist-high. The slug hits the hound in the head, just as it takes off ... and no more dog. The smack of the bullet knocks it almost two yards along the drive, and the slack-boned heap tells its own story.

If there is a doggy heaven, that one is already there.

175

I want to puke.

Instead, I swallow my guts, and say, 'Look – these gates ... they could be linked.'

'What's that?' Jones diverts his attention from Sagar and the big man just long enough to ask the question.

'They could be alarmed,' I say. 'To the house ... to anywhere.'

The big man growls, 'Don't worry about little things, Martin. Save all your worries for the safe.'

And, by now, the gate is unlocked.

We open the gate and move into the grounds. We pause long enough to take the gun from the guard's holster, then move at a crouched run – single file – along the grass bordering the path.

I come last, and I am so damn anxious about what might be following us that I collide with the side of a tree. That's me, folks ... always good for a laugh.

3.05 a.m. (G.M.T.)...

We are at the door – the door of the giant's castle – which, presumably, is where we want to be ... but it is not, necessarily, where *I* want to be. I can think of a thousand and one more comfortable places – a thousand and one more welcoming places – and that not counting beds. That I am still perpendicular amazes me. I am no hero. I should have passed out, some hours back. Come to think of it, I am certifiable ... I *should* have passed out, and saved myself all this high-pressure anguish.

Guns. I hate guns. Guns are made, specifically, to kill people with ... and there are too many guns around here for comfort. I could get myself killed – and just because I hadn't the gumption to pass out, when I was able ... sweet Jesus, I *must* be certifiable.

Dilton-Emmet grabs me, and drags me to one side of the

176

door. He pushes me behind his cliff-side bulk, then hefts his Luger in a very businesslike manner.

At which point, I pee myself ... and see no reason at all to apologise.

Jones presses the bell-push, and we wait.

The big man whispers, 'Stay low, Martin. Out of the firing line,' as if I need advice or encouragement.

The door opens and a man, dressed in butler's uniform stands illuminated by the light from the hall. He is a big man. In ordinary circumstances, he would be a handful ... but these are not ordinary circumstances.

He knows the rules of this very rough game.

Jones smiles at him and places the forefinger of his left hand against his lips as a gesture of silence. The butler guy tries to nod his complete understanding – he tries to nod, but can't ... the silencered snout of Jones's Luger is holding his chin a little too high.

Sagar steps out, from alongside the door, passes Jones, checks that the hall is empty, then smacks the butler across the back of the neck with his gun. Exit one butler.

As we enter the house, Jones says, 'Two more servants. Root them out, Sagar. Deal with them, then join us.'

Sagar grunts, 'Okay,' and cat-foots his way towards some stairs.

Jones, Dilton-Emmet and myself go into the house. The man-mountain with the whiskers knows his manners ... he closes the door, very gently, when we are all inside.

3.10 a.m. (G.M.T.)...

It is all over, bar the shouting. Bar the cheering. Bar the safe-breaking.

The servants have all been 'dealt with' – the expression used ... and that expression covers mileage of which I dare not even contemplate. The trio of madmen are, once more, a compact trio and we face the man who (presumably) made this cockeyed journey necessary.

The man.

The man watches ... the man, his wife and his teenage daughter. His face is pale and expressionless, except for the eyes. The eyes blaze with the fire of fanaticism. His wife is afraid – a little afraid ... and, although she tries, she cannot hide her fear. As for the daughter? Dear God, the daughter! ... in her jeans and tie-dyed shirt, she represents her kind; the conviction of youth; their conviction of immortality; their certainty that, although they, themselves, are justified in inflicting terror they are, at the same time, incapable of being terrorised.

Poor, deluded youth ... and, suddenly, I am reminded of Anne.

I plead, 'Look – for God's sake ...'

'Shut up!'

The two words are like a double whip-crack – as cold, and vicious, as *that* – and Jones doesn't even grant me the simple courtesy of shifting his eyes from the waiting trio.

Willie Sagar growls, 'Keep out of it, Martin. The safe ... that's all you're here for.'

'Martin?' The man speaks, for the first time. He has a cultured voice; a slight drawl – a voice very much like Jones's voice – and, as he makes a question of my name, a quick, cat-smile touches his lips.

'That's my name, sir,' I say, gently ... and the 'sir' comes quite naturally and unconsciously.

'Andrew Martin. The thief,' he replies, and there is genuine interest in his voice. He glances momentarily at the stain in front of my trousers, and adds, 'A thief ... but not a violent person.'

'He knows you, Martin,' growls the big man. 'He knows us all. It's his job to know.'

'He certainly knows me,' says Jones, coldly.

'I should.' The cat-smile comes and goes, again. 'We

178

were at school together. Fifth form, and Remove, as I recall.'

'We didn't like each other ... even in those days.'

The man nods, and says, 'We were too *much* alike.'

'Probably.' Jones dismisses the conversation, nods at an excellent reproduction of Gainsborough's *Watering Place*, and says, 'The safe's behind that, Martin. Get to work.'

'Without even having to search,' murmurs the man.

Jones says, 'You, too, have your traitors ... didn't you know?'

3.15 a.m. (G.M.T.)...

Jones is right ... but, of course. Behind the hinged Gainsborough there is a safe. A good safe; a German safe, made from good German steel. It is a dial-operated job and, for this, I give due thanks.

Don't let the fiction boys fool you. Stethoscopes and super-sensitive ears do *not* tease secrets from dial-operated safes; those tumblers fall very softly, and only a fraction of an inch ... they make no noise whatever. But, if you can get *at* them, you can feel them fall.

Above the dial ... that is the place.

I am, for the moment, treading my own territory. I know what I am about. I am practising my own trade, and I need neither guns nor violence for that trade.

I open my case of picklocks, choose a drill-bit, then examine the face of the safe very carefully, before I decide where the hole must go. To a certain extent it is hit-and-miss; I know English safes, but German safes ... they may have secrets I have yet to learn.

The diamond tip moves into the metal, and I allow myself a quick smile of satisfaction as the purr of the tiny electric drill alters key, slightly. Different metal – different

179

resistance ... I am eating my way through the tumblers themselves.

I go all the way through, then remove the drill, take it to pieces and replace each part in the case.

Then, comes the probe-work. Tiny probes – made with a perfection which makes dental probes look like crowbars ... and I turn the dial, figure at a time.

At the right numbers, I feel the tumblers drop. I have the numbers ... three – five – seven – eight. All I need, now, is their correct order. There is more probe-work – less than five minutes – and I have done what I am here for.

Eight, five, seven, three.

I remove the probes. Spin the dial, then move the numbers to the correct sequence. I turn the handle, and the safe opens.

Easy!

I step aside and allow the big man to collect papers, envelopes, books and God knows what else, and stuff them into the blouse of his windcheater.

3.25 a.m. (G.M.T.) ...

The man says, 'What good will it do, Jones?'

'We'll know a little more.'

'Quite ... but, what *good* will it do?'

'A little.'

'It won't stop anything. It won't *change* anything.'

'A little,' repeats Jones, softly.

They are talking above my head. Double-talk. Talk which means far more than the words say; talk with overtones of horror.

Jones says, 'Your hatchetmen may become afraid.'

'I doubt it.'

'They're human.'

'They have a cause.'

'Of course. A hundred causes ... but *some* may become afraid.'

But for the three silencered Lugers, it might be an academic conversation; a difference of opinion between two highly intelligent men. But, the Lugers make it something else. The Lugers are all-important. *They* are the argument ... the final, clinching argument.

I want to say something, but I can't. I can't find the words ... and I can't find the words, because I'm damned if I know what's going on.

The man drawls, 'Granting the possibility of fear – that some will become afraid – what does it achieve?'

'Enough,' says Jones. 'Enough, and they'll *all* be afraid.'

'It's a poor premise.'

'Your premise,' counters Jones. 'The premise of every terrorist.'

'Not terrorists, Jones. Freedom fighters.'

'Ah, yes. But whose freedom?'

'Not mine, it would seem,' says the man, and there is a touch of sadness in his voice.

'Not yours,' agrees Jones.

The man's wife breathes, 'For God's sake! Get it over with.'

'Gently, my love.' The man smiles infinite fondness at his wife. 'You carry my name. Hold it proudly.'

She bites her lip, and nods, dumbly.

The man turns to Jones, and says, 'This small fiasco. What will it achieve?'

'Who knows?' Jones moves his shoulder. It is almost a gesture of boredom. 'One less hi-jacking, perhaps. One less fool ready to plant a bomb, and kill innocents.'

'It's a gamble, Jones.'

'Of course ... but you won't see the turn of the card.'

'Unfortunately.' The man hesitates, then says, 'My wife. My child. Would it be a waste of time if ...'

'A complete waste of time,' cuts in Jones. 'They know

what you are. Who you are. They'd merely continue, where you left off ... and with the additional threat of personal anger.'

'You were always very logical,' sighs the man.

And – dammit – now I *know*. This is a killing. A 'hit'. A 'wasting'. A 'contract'. What the hell fancy name they use for cold-blooded murder these days ... this is *it*. And, I'm part of it, and I *want* no part of it. This is not my bag – not my thing ... I am a thief, not a killer.

If I could run, I would run. But, where the hell do I run to?

The man says, 'May I kiss my wife and child?'

Jones nods his head in sardonic permission. It is almost the mockery of a bow.

The man holds out his arms, and his wife moves into them. Their lips meet ... and then he turns, suddenly.

From somewhere – presumably from some hiding place in the back of his wife's dress – he has taken a pistol. Little more than a deadly toy. A .22 – a woman's gun – and no match for the three Lugers which are trained upon this tiny family. It is, at once, a gesture of defiance and a last attempt to kill the man who is about to order his destruction ... a useless gesture, and a lost attempt.

. Dilton-Emmet tilts his Luger, squeezes the trigger and the toy pistol explodes and sends its tiny slug into the floor-boards as the man spins and staggers, then clutches his shattered shoulder.

Dilton-Emmet growls, 'That's not in the book of rules, old son. And *I'm* not your old school chum.'

For the rest, it is horror, piled upon horror.

Jones nods. It is almost an off-handed movement of the head.

Dilton-Emmet takes the wife, and Sagar takes the daughter. The wife's knuckle of her right forefinger has just reached her teeth, to hold back a forbidden scream of fear, as the first of three slugs tears her flesh and sends her tumbling into an obscenely unnatural heap against a bullet-slashed armchair. The girl jerks her jaw high, in defiance ... then she, too, dies with less dignity than a beast at an abattoir.

And *now*...!

The fury boils up, inside me. The fury, the disgust, the outrage ... the plain, honest, decent *hatred*. For a moment – for one brilliant, never-to-be-forgotten moment – I don't give a damn about my own life. To die means nothing – *nothing* – if, in return, I can tear the throat from one of these murdering bastards, and take him to hell with me. I clench my fists, convulsively.

Then, Willie Sagar says, 'Don't!' and his Luger is touching my side, just above the belt.

The heroic moment passes. I embrace cowardice, open my fingers and allow my held breath to escape in a single rush.

There is something approaching compassion in Sagar's tone, as he voices what he must believe is the final argument.

Softly – almost gently – he says, 'Innocent people – women and kids ... they've taken a lot longer to die.'

I breathe, 'Yeah.' But, I am not *quite* convinced.

The final act has still to be played and, to my eternal shame, I am hypnotised into watching, by the sheer magnificence of its mockery of civilised conduct.

The man stands and waits. He ignores the bloody bundles which, a few seconds before, were his wife and daughter. He must be in agony; the bones of his shoulder *must* be smashed, and his jacket shows a growing blossom of scarlet. The blood trickles in rivulets, like a crimson delta, down the back of his hand, and drips from the tips of his fingers onto the carpet.

He flicks a glance at my face, and what he sees there brings the quick, cat smile to his lips.

His voice is quite controlled, as he says, 'You really must

steel yourself, Martin. These things happen. Your government – most governments – delude themselves. Delude the people. But, this *is* war ... and we, in this room, know that simple fact. We face truth, Martin. Truth ... however unpleasant. War. And this particular battle has been won by your friends. But, fortunately, that's all it is. An isolated battle. Not victory.'

Jones raises his Luger.

In an equally controlled – equally unhurried – voice, he murmurs, 'When you're ready.'

Godammit, they are like perfectly mannered *gentlemen*. At this moment they are the greatest argument for and, at the same time, the greatest argument against, the public school system. They are inhuman ... but superb. They are without feeling ... but also without fear. They are sub-human ... but, at the same time, they are *super*-human.

The man drawls, 'At your convenience, Jones.'

Jones tightens his finger around the trigger of the Luger. The pistol pop-pop-pops his chuckle of destruction ... and the room suddenly has the smell of cordite ... and the sweet stench of newly spilled blood.

SIX ...

The Jeep rejoins the outskirts of the city, and carries us back to the airport. The uniformed goon opens the rear gate, for our entrance and, once more, raises his arm in a stupid salute. The plane is ready and, within minutes, we are airborne and heading for home.

The three of them sit together and, with the aid of a torch, examine the papers and documents taken from the safe. They seem satisfied ... almost pleased.

Me?

I find a place, well away from them, settle as well as I can in my still-damp pants, and do some very heavy thinking.

It isn't *on* ... that, for a start. That, for a base-line. Louse, I may be – thief, I most certainly am ... even other, and worse, things. But *this* ...

Damn it to hell, we are not at war. *We are not at war.* Were we at war, it might be different. Were we at war, medals might have been won – medals might have been deserved – *but, we are not at war.*

Okay – I also know the counter-arguments ... tell that to the poor sods who've had their guts shot away by terrorists. Tell it to the torture victims. Tell it to the hostages. Tell it to the passengers on a hi-jacked plane. Tell it to the innocents in the way of a car-bomb. Tell it to the thousands of already dead – victims of terrorism – tell it to the tens of thousands who make up their weeping next-of-kin ... *but, we are not at war.*

And, whilever we are not at war, Jones, Dilton-Emmet, Willie Sagar and however many others there are of their kind are merely *our* terrorists. That's all. They perform abominations which, when others perform those same abominations, disgust ordinary, decent people. And, damn it, they perform those abominations without feeling. Without shame ... yes, even with pride.

Pride!

They take pride in doing their work well ... which means doing it without mercy. They kill without compassion. In cold blood. Without even *thinking*.

And yet, they are proud. They have honour.

I feel drowsy. Two nights, without sleep – the tension of the last few hours – the gradual release of the tension – the slow lowering of fear ... it all combines.

But, as my eyes droop – as sleep creeps in – I mumble to myself.

'Nothing secret was ever honourable ... nothing secret was ever honourable ... nothing secret ... was ever ... honourable ...'

SEVEN...

We are back in Newman Street; back in the crummy office with its jumble-sale desk and its quintet of unmatched chairs. I am sitting on one of these chairs. Jones, too, is using one of the chairs. Sagar is performing what seems to be his favourite trick – using the closed door as a leaning-post – and Dilton-Emmet has hoisted his arse onto a corner of the desk.

This is (presumably) some sort of mild celebration.

The toast – if it is a toast – is being made in good class brandy, and I see no reason why, merely because I despise this trio of kill-happy untouchables, I should not drink and enjoy good booze ... by my own reckoning, I've earned it.

'We got you back in one piece,' says Jones, mildly.

I growl, 'Forgive me if I'm ungrateful. I didn't even want to go.'

'You made it possible.'

'Yeah. But, had I known ...'

'What?' rumbles the big man.

I taste brandy, then say, 'You wouldn't even understand.'

'Try us,' suggests Jones, with a smile.

'That you're killers. Thugs. That you're ...'

'We'll accept that – as a compliment, if you like ... but, what else?'

'You butchered a man, his wife, his daughter. You destroyed ...'

'Ah! But *you* identified him, for us,' murmurs Jones.

'Unintentionally.'

Sagar says, 'No ... *fortunately.*'

'I'm damned if I go along with *that* ...'

'He was one of three,' cuts in Jones.

186

'So you've explained.' There is harsh mockery in my voice.

'Athens, Cologne and Madrid. That was where . . .'

'I know the words. You've sung the song before.'

'And *you* don't like the tune?' Jones's voice hardens.

'I think it's over-rated. When you deliberately murder a man, and . . .'

'In Cologne it was a widower and his two daughters. In Madrid it was a man, his wife, his two sons and his mother-in-law. What the hell you call it, Martin, *we* call it success.'

'Holy Christ!'

'It *shows* them. It's a demonstration . . . one they'll understand.'

Tempers are fraying at the edges. Sagar is scowling his disapproval. Dilton-Emmet is watching my face, with all the eager anticipation of a caged cat eyeing the approach of a nice juicy steak. Jones pauses long enough to tip what remains of his brandy down his throat.

He says, 'Drink up, Martin. You'll need more than one drink to take what I'm going to tell you.'

I drink up. It is still good booze.

Dilton-Emmet moves from the desk, re-fills Jones's glass, then mine, then returns to the desk and resumes his watching.

Jones starts slowly. He has the facts – and, strangely, I do not doubt that they *are* facts – and he presents them, much as a scientist might present a tested formula to a class of understanding students. With the same clinical certainty. With the same calm, unhurried expertise of the master imparting knowledge to a pupil.

He says, 'Check with the back numbers of any newspaper, Martin. The biggest illegal arms cache *ever* . . . Bayswater. Here, in London. The hide-out of the so-called "Carlos". A known, freelance terrorist.

'The P.L.O. It's a rich organisation – a near-legal multi-national company. Check it out ... it has fifty million pounds invested in the United Kingdom, alone. Respectable? The Libyan Embassy, in Athens – Athens, for obvious reasons – has an office. It makes no pretence. An embassy, no less, with an office as a recruiting centre for would-be terrorists. Respectable? Arafat – remember when he was granted right of audience in the United Nations Assembly? The P.L.O. offices in Beirut received congratulatory telegrams from almost a dozen separate terrorist organisations – "officially" unconnected with the P.L.O. ... the mark of respectability?

'The Popular Front – the subsidiary of the P.L.O., Arafat's own organisation – hi-jacked the Lufthansa aircraft. It required three months of planning, by at least four separate terrorist organisations. The Yemen was their "safe" landing spot. The ransom asked for – and paid – was five million pounds. Respectable?

'The destruction of the Gulf Refinery, at Rotterdam – March 1971 – the Jihaz al-Rasd group ... the P.L.O undercover boys. Respectable?

'The bomb attack, in Jerusalem – thirteen dead, sixty-two wounded – July, 1975 – P.L.O. planned ... respectable? The bombs of Belfast – the bombs of London – the bombs of Birmingham ... respectable? The reported words of a spokesman of the Baader-Meinhof organisation – "We are all used and we must all expect to be used" ... respectable? The reported words of Ahmed Yamani – one of the Popular Front leaders – "Terror is just another form of psychological warfare" ... respectable? The words of Arafat, himself – "We teach terror in the classroom" ... respectable? Habash – "The main thing is to have people always *expecting* terrorism" ... respectable? Gun-running ... respectable? Dope-running ... respectable? Blackmail ... respectable? Hi-jacking ... respectable? My God, man, what yardstick do you use for your precious "respectability"?'

I sip my brandy, curl my lips, and mock, 'You've left out the I.R.A.'

'They aren't important. They're just about the smallest cog in the whole terrorist machine. They're a front. A façade. They attract attention. They keep London "safe". Everybody's looking for Irishmen ... while the other groups plan their next atrocity.'

'If you're right...' I begin.

'I'm right, Martin.' His voice is heavy with disgust. He says, 'I don't *like* being their opposite number ... but it's the only diplomacy they understand. You can't talk to them – you can't argue with them ... you can only kill 'em. It's taken years – years, and hell knows how many innocent lives – for my own masters to accept that unpalatable truth ... that the only way to handle a man who deals in fear is to make *him* frightened. That's what last night was about. And Cologne. And Madrid. There were more than a hundred raids, during the early hours of this morning – "safe houses", named on the lists from that deed box ... it'll halt them, for a while, in the U.K. ... no more.' He suddenly sounds weary, and not far from despair and, for a moment I feel something akin to sympathy. He ends, 'For a while – for a short while – until they re-group ... then, it's back to the start-line. Searching for the new lists. Identifying the newly promoted top men. The new couriers. The new "safe" houses. Everything!'

'The Forth Bridge,' I murmur.

'Eh?'

'Painting.'

'Ah! ... quite.' He passes me a wry smile.

'Otherwise,' growls the big man, 'the bridge collapses.'

Nobody speaks for a few moments; we sip brandy and each man lives with his own private thoughts.

Me? I'm as near convinced as I'll ever be. I've been told facts; some of the facts I already know, and remember ... the others can be checked, if necessary. Whatever else he is,

Jones is no fool, which means he hasn't lied. Why should he tell lies which can be proved to be lies? The truth, then. Snippets of truth, which can be put together and which, when they *are* put together, reveal a massive truth. A world-wide truth. A terrifying truth.

A war ... a secret, underground war. A *world* war, of which much of the world is unaware. Not a war of trenches, of blitzkriegs or even of guerilla fighting. Not even a war of ideologies. A war, without armies, in the conventional sense ... but, nevertheless, a war with enemies and allies. Basically – trite though it sounds – a war between good and evil ... and, not even *that*. A war, in the final analysis, between *evil* and *evil*. To fight the devil *with* the devil. To fight terror with counter-terror.

And, this bloody shambles we have the gall to call 'civilisation'.

For no real reason, I am curious ... morbidly curious.

In little more than a whisper, I ask, 'How many?'

'What?' Jones surfaces from his reverie.

'Killings? How many people have you killed? *Had* to kill?'

Jones shrugs.

Sagar grunts, 'We don't keep a tally.'

'This little lot started with Rawle,' says Dilton-Emmet.

'Rawle!' I am surprised. I have little cause for surprise; it is far too logical for surprise.

Jones says, 'He knew about the deed box. The lists. That's why.'

'Yes, but ...'

'In the hands of the wrong man ...'

'Yeah – I realise that – but ...'

'Certain well-informed criminals know of their existence,' says Jones, slowly. 'The wise ones leave it at that. They *know* ... but they keep even their knowledge a secret. The fools – the Rawles – have dreams. They argue – rightly – that the lists are worth a king's ransom. Blackmail. Safe ...

and with an open cheque. That's their dream. It was Rawle's dream.'

'Noble?' I ask. 'The Jew? The jeweller?'

'He knew ... of course he knew.'

'In that case, why not...'

'A balancing act, Martin.' Jones's smile is crooked and cynical. 'The usual tightrope. It had to look like a straight jewel-theft. Noble wouldn't tell the police about the deed box ... but the murder of Noble might have alerted Noble's friends. Therefore, Noble had to be allowed to live ... but kept incommunicado. Special Branch officers – acting as normal investigating detectives – pulled the trick ... the statement he was "asked" to make kept him busy, and away from a telephone, long enough for us to act.'

'Every angle,' I say, admiringly.

Dilton-Emmet said, 'We damn near shot you. It was the spin of a coin, old son.'

'Why the hell...'

'Then we found we needed you.' Jones sounds almost bored. 'You bought your life with the skill we required in Athens.'

I stare at him, and say, 'Well, thank *you*.'

'We let you run loose for most of the day. Followed, of course.'

'Eh?'

'To give you the rope. To see what you did with it. Whether you made it into a noose, or not.'

'Oh! Ah – yes ... of course.'

'You didn't,' smiles Jones.

'Fortunately.'

'Quite.'

'You could have had my word,' I assure him.

'Not good enough, I'm afraid.'

Dilton-Emmet chuckles, and says, 'You're a cunning devil, Martin ... the way you shifted the opposition, yesterday morning.'

'Yesterday morning?' I frown ... 'yesterday morning' is a lifetime in the past.

'The Capri. It was waiting for you, when you arrived home.'

'Oh ... *that*?'

'It was a neat trick. Phoning the cops.'

'You really *were* keeping tabs,' I remark.

'Those two.' The big man shakes his head, and grins at the memory. 'We raced them – that bloody car – all over London. They had a suspicion – y'know ... that we were on the move. We beat 'em to Rawle's place. And to Burnt Oak. But they beat *us* to your place ... and, just for a few minutes, it looked as if we'd come unstuck.'

That's how it comes out. As simple as that. As sloppy – as off-handedly – as casually as *that*!

Something, the size and texture of a cricket ball, lodges in my throat. For a moment, I can't speak. Can't breathe. Can't *believe*.

Then, I whisper, 'Burnt ... Burnt Oak?'

'Your pal's place,' amplifies the big man, cheerfully.

'Y'mean...' I choke on the words. 'Y'mean Len? That *you* are the bastards who...'

In a very mild voice, Jones says, 'Don't get excited, Martin.'

'Excited? *Excited!* What the hell sort of people *are* you? What you did to Len was...'

'We couldn't trust him.'

'*Trust him.* He was the most trustworthy – the most honest – man in the whole bloody world. He was – he was...'

'We hadn't a hold over him,' says Jones, flatly. 'Nothing ... therefore, he wasn't trustworthy.'

'You bastards,' I moan. 'Oh, you bastards ... you bloody *animals*.'

With zero emotion, Jones continues, 'Circumstances demanded that we got whatever information he had in his possession. After that ... we had to make sure he didn't pass that information on to others.' He pauses, then adds, 'It doesn't apply to you, Martin. We *have* a hold over you – thanks to Rawle ... we have the body of your wife, and the knife you stabbed her with. From our point of view, you're – er – "safe".'

I mutter, 'Oh, my God!'

I push myself up from the chair and move, like a drunken man, for the door.

Jones's voice drones on, 'We have you, Martin. Don't forget that. Ever! Whichever way you turn, you're in the net. Otherwise *you* wouldn't be alive.'

I want to spew. I want to die. I want out. *Out.*

As I open the door to leave, I fight for air and groan, 'Oh ... my ... God...'

PART THREE

THE KILL

It is not necessary to choose any particular time of the year for giving the dogs
a hunt for rats.

RAT

The Harmsworth Encylopaedia

ONE...

There she was. Twisted, boneless and stupid; with her skirt ruffled up, above her thighs, and with one leg of her stocking-tights badly torn at the knee; with one mule missing, and the other hanging to its foot by the toe; with her eyes wide, and her mouth still fighting for a last breath she couldn't suck in.

There she was – twisted, boneless and stupid ... and very dead.

TWO...

Despite all the carnage I'd witnessed during the last twenty-four hours, that mental image was still there. Anne, at her moment of strangulation. All the other things surrounded it – were an interwoven design, which framed it ... were horrific, but of a lesser degree, and unimportant, by comparison.

I wandered the streets, carrying that image with me.

God knows where I went. Leicester Square – I remember Leicester Square, and *The Talk of the Town*, and one part of my mind registering the star billing, and thinking what a fine night out it would be ... what a fine night out it *might* have been. And Aldwych ... a passing cab brushing the skirt of my jacket, in Aldwych, and the passing thought that I'd been less than a yard from the only *real* solution.

Other than that – other than Leicester Square and Aldwych – God knows.

It must be possible to walk a thousand miles, never walk

along the same street twice, and still stay in London. There are streets, and streets, and streets – miles, and miles, and miles ... and thousands of pavements, with millions of corners. No man need ever be other than lonely, in London. For sheer solitude, it makes the Sahara seem overcrowded. I tell you ... people, not sand, make a desert.

I know. You have my word ... I *know*! I walked, until darkness fell – north, south, east and west – God only knows where I walked, or how far I walked ... seeking a single oasis.

I found nothing.

Any tart – any down-and-out – any junkie – any wino – any last dreg from the whole of humanity would have sufficed, but I found *nothing* ... and, throughout every second of my wandering, a looped film flickered through the projector of my brain.

There she was. Twisted, boneless and stupid...

THREE...

I walked through the door, because it looked familiar. That's all ... a sort of reflex action. And, it wasn't until I was into the foyer, with the manager talking to me, and calling me 'sir', that I realised that I actually *owned* the place; that I was in my own casino, at Hammersmith.

He was saying, '... and the police, I'm afraid, sir.'

'Eh?'

I screwed my mind into a tight ball of concentration, forced myself to listen, and forced the words to make sense.

He coughed, frowned his concern, and said, 'This – er – gentleman, sir.'

'Which gentleman?'

'He's an American gentleman. He's been asking to see you.'

'American?'

'Albert – Albert Barlow ... he's very anxious to see you, sir.'

'Albert?'

'Yes, sir. He's in the lounge bar. He's been...'

'You're sure his name's *Albert*?'

'Oh, yes. Albert Barlow. He's...'

'Close shop,' I snapped.

'Sir?'

'You heard me. Close shop. Everybody out ... except Barlow.'

The manager eyed me with some solicitude, and said, 'Mr Martin, are you ill?'

'No.'

'You look ... unwell,' he ventured.

'Are you a doctor?' I asked, tightly.

'No, sir. Of course not, but...'

'Okay. When you're qualified, give an opinion ... and then, only if I ask for it. Meanwhile, get this place cleared.'

'I – I can't see how...'

'I don't give a damn how. Get it cleared. Everybody ... with the exception of Barlow. Give 'em their money back. Anything. But get it cleared.'

He still hesitated then, before I could give him a full broadside, he frowned, and muttered, 'Mr Martin – er – the police...'

'Sod the police.'

'I'm sorry, sir, but they made me give them my assurance.'

'What about?'

'They – they want to see you, sir. Urgently.'

'Is that a fact?'

'They made me promise. If you called in here, to let them know.'

'Later,' I snapped.

'Sir, I – I gave them my solemn word...'

'Look.' I forced what I fondly believed to be a friendly smile to settle on my lips. I said, 'Okay – you send for the police ... that's understood. I know what it's about ... and that it's important. But, get this place cleared, first. Let me have this Barlow character alone, for about fifteen minutes. Then, send for the police ... I'll still be here.'

He looked worried. Undecided.

'For old time's sake,' I pleaded.

'I – I dunno. The police were...'

'*Sod the police!*' I exploded. 'This is still my place. You owe me some sort of loyalty. Get it cleared. Customers, staff – everybody ... except the Barlow hound. Tell *him* I'm on my way. Then, come back to your office. I'll be waiting. Now, go to it – don't argue ... bloody-well *do* it.'

He stammered, 'Yes ... yes, sir,' and almost ran from the foyer, into the body of the building.

FOUR...

I damn near prayed. I'm not a praying man – I don't go for the dear-God-I'm-up-shit-creek-please-send-me-a-paddle routine ... but I damn near prayed.

All I wanted was time. A few minutes – no more ... after that, they could throw me to the lions. I was past caring. Past feeling. Past *everything* ... except that one wish.

It had to be *him*. For Christ's sake, coincidence wasn't *that* cockeyed. There couldn't be two 'Alberts' – both Yanks – both anxious to meet the husband of my once-upon-a-time wife.

It had to be him!

I sat in the manager's office, and waited. I took deep breaths, to get the oxygen moving around in my blood stream. I forced my mind to forget; to eliminate the last couple of days from my life, and to pick up the beat at some point before the break-in – before the Athens trip – before my whole world had tilted and gone crazy. It took some doing, but a triple whisky – neat – steadied things, nicely.

I relaxed. I even tried to touch my toes a couple of times; flexed my arms and legs, like a downhill racer preparing for the 'off'. I didn't know what the hell I was going to meet – a giant or a runt, a kid or an oldster – but, regardless of size or age, he was going to bleed. He was going to hurt; some of the hurt I'd carried around with me for far too long was due to be transferred to this unknown creep who'd entered my life, and who'd now crossed the Atlantic to be at the receiving end of a thumping.

And, my Christ, what a thumping!

I clenched and unclenched my fists. I mentally ran over all the dirty tricks of rough-house scrapping I'd ever indulged in, or witnessed. I loosened my tie a little, and unfastened the top button of my shirt, to give my throat room to expand and take in air. I fastened my jacket, to ensure that it wouldn't flap, and give this 'Albert' bastard something which he might grab.

Then, I finished the drink, and waited.

The manager still looked worried, when he returned to the office.

'Everybody gone?' I asked.

He nodded, miserably.

'Including the staff?'

'Yes.'

'Barlow's still waiting?'

'Yes, sir. I told him you'd be joining him, very shortly.'

'Very shortly,' I agreed, grimly.

He moistened his dry lips, and said, 'Mr Martin, the police...'

'Fifteen minutes. Then send for 'em.'

'I – I could be in trouble, sir.'

'Trouble?'

'For not – for not...'

'They're sloppy,' I said, gently. 'They should have had a man here, waiting. They're sloppy ... they can't blame you for that.'

'They – they trusted me ... that's all.'

I smiled a not-too-nice smile, and said, 'They'll learn by their mistake, won't they?'

'Mr Martin, I think...'

'While I'm here, *I* do the thinking.'

'Yes, sir. But – y'know ... I might be in trouble.'

'Stay behind me,' I said, sardonically. 'You'll be an eye-witness to what trouble *really* means.' I stood up from the chair, waved a hand at the bottle, and said, 'Sit down, mate. Stop worrying. See how drunk you can get, in fifteen minutes.'

He sighed, 'Yes, sir,' and lowered himself wearily into the chair.

As I reached the door, I turned, and said, 'Thanks.' ... And I meant it.

FIVE ...

I didn't hurry. There was no reason to hurry. I walked at a normal, unhurried speed, from the manager's office, down the stairs, along the corridors and into the bar.

He was there, at the bar, sipping some sort of nancy-boy's booze. Waiting, and quite composed.

I eyed him, and sized him up as I approached. We were about of an age; not young, not old; maybe in our prime ... maybe just a little past our prime. He had a bit of a gut which, I calculated, equalled out my loss of sleep. He had a jaw – a certain arrogance about the way he held himself – which might have worried me a little, had it not been for the furnace of blind fury which I was keeping bottled up, inside. Okay – he was going to be a handful ... but my hands were more than ready for him.

I eyed him, as I approached, along the carpet of the deserted lounge bar ... and he, in turn, eyed me.

I joined him at the bar-counter, turned, and we watched each other through the tinted glass, beyond the shelf of bottles.

'Martin?' he said.

'Yeah.' I nodded at his reflection. 'You'll be "Albert".'

'Albert Barlow.'

'I never asked about the second name. It wasn't important.'

'No?' He drained his drink, placed the glass on the bar-counter, then said, 'It's Barlow.'

'Big deal,' I murmured.

He said, 'I've travelled a long way to meet you, Martin.'

'It would seem,' I agreed, gently.

'I'm a busy man.'

'Pinkerton ... and all that.'

'You know?'

Still keeping my voice gentle, and under control, I said, 'I've heard things.'

'I,' he said, 'would *like* to hear things.'

'Ask around. You might be lucky.'

'I've already asked around.'

'And?'

'The Limey cops keep a very tight mouth.'

'So-o ... you're out of luck. Right? ... "Albert"?'

'I wouldn't push things too far,' he warned, softly.

'No?'

'This "Albert" thing – the way you say it ... I don't find it funny.'

'There's no extra charge for not laughing ... "Albert".'

'I'm warning you, Martin.'

'That, too?' I sneer, quietly.

'What's that mean?'

'Warning me ... on top of shafting the arse out of my wife.'

'Look...'

'No! *You* look ... "Albert".' I turned to face him, and let him have it, full blast. 'Listen – and listen good – because there'll be no encores to this particular monologue. You started trouble, fink. You! The minute you couldn't control your bloody fly-zip, that's when I started having problems. Until then, things were riding nice and smoothly. But you elbowed your cock-happy way into the act and, from that moment, I've lived with grief. You name the brand ... I've lived with it. And, my fine feathered bastard, I've wanted to meet up with you ever since. Muriel was mine. Mine! And we'll start from that simple fact. She was never yours – she was never anybody's ... always *mine*. Don't give yourself any medals, "Albert". The only good thing you ever did was cross the Atlantic. This way, it saves me money. I can still knock seven shades of shit out of you ... and save myself the air-fare.'

As he unbuttoned his jacket, he growled, 'That, I doubt.'

'That,' I rasped, 'is about to be demonstrated.'

He was a mug. He left himself open for the most important thump of the whole game ... the first. This wasn't a Queensberry Rules thing. This was a damn good hiding; a smash-up, till one of us couldn't even crawl. And the mug pinned his own arms with the sleeves of his jacket.

I brought a right, from about knee-height, and meant it to explode right on the button. It didn't. He saw it, a split second before it arrived, twisted and killed most of the power with his shoulder.

Nevertheless, it sprawled him and, as he went down, he scissored his legs, and brought me down, too. I rolled clear of the leg-hold, smacked the top of my skull against the leg of one of the tables, and realised something ... this bull was going to take some de-horning.

We climbed upright, together – about two yards apart – and he'd rid himself of the encumbrance of the jacket.

We circled a couple of times, then rushed. He was seeking judo holds. I wasn't ... I was seeking somewhere to hit, and somewhere to cripple.

He rode a second swing, grabbed the wrist and arm, turned and put on the pressure. I knew damn well my arm was going – that the bones would never again be nearer breaking, without actually snapping – so, I bent against the pressure, wrapped my free fingers around a bar-stool leg, and let him have it with the edge of the seat. I aimed good, and I aimed hard; midway, between the ankle and the knee ... smack onto the shin-bone. He yelped with pain, and the pressure on my held arm eased enough for me to yank it clear.

As we parted I let the bar-stool have a return swing. Head-high. It could have decapitated him ... but it didn't. He ducked, then came in low and slammed a punch home, below my belt. That, too, hurt, and I let go of the stool and heard the crash of the mirror and bottles, from behind the bar.

Then, for all of three minutes, it was toe-to-toe work. Real, honest-to-God, bare-knuckle cow-kicking. We took some stick, and we gave some stick. This fink was no she-man, and I'd enough hatred swirling around inside me to ignore the pasting he was giving me, in order to return the compliment with (I hoped) interest. I belted that face until it puffed, then split, then bled and I, too, could feel the bomb-blasts, as they exploded; I could taste the blood from split lips and a smashed nose, I could feel the loosened teeth and one eye was closing, fast.

For the moment, we were animals – rogue males – fighting out a claim for a female ... and the fact that the female was long dead didn't matter, and wasn't even thought of.

We hammered and thumped until our arms were weary, then we stepped apart, to regain our strength.

He was the first to come forward, again, and I met him with a vicious kick, aimed at the groin. I mistimed, slightly, and he half-turned, and the toe of my shoe caught him under the knee-cap.

He gasped, tried to put weight on the leg, then went down on one knee, and gasped again as the knee hit the floor.

I had him!

I came in from the rear, clamped a forearm across the front of his throat, and drove my own knee into the nape of his neck. No rules, you understand ... just smash, and keep smashing, until the other was pulp. He was mine; there wasn't a damn thing he could do. The more he twisted, the tighter I made the pressure. The more he clawed backwards with his flaying arms, the harder I pressed and the harder I pulled. His neck must have been made of tyre-rubber ... otherwise, I'd have torn his head from his shoulders.

He was getting weaker. I could feel it. I could feel the weight of him dragging on my arm and, any second, he was due to go under. Unconscious ... maybe dead. And, ask me if *I* cared which.

I relaxed my hold, just as he toppled and, as he sprawled, I put the boot in. Hard. Scientifically. With maximum accuracy. In the ribs. In the side of the neck. Full-face. Into the gut. I had him, and I meant to keep him; he was horizontal and, if I had anything to do with it, he wasn't going to be perpendicular for one hell of a long time.

In retrospect, I think I would have killed him. Indeed, I don't think I was worried about whether, or not, I was already kicking a corpse.

That was the state of my mind. That was the degree of my anger. This man – this 'thing' – was the cause of it all. I'd been happy until *he'd* shoved his finger into my life but, since then, I'd been miserable, frightened, frustrated ... yes, and even, in a way, crazy.

Because of *this* bastard!

So, why the hell should I care whether, or not, I was kicking the life out of him?

Why the hell should I *care*?

I didn't kill him. I merely crippled him, but he lived. The manager didn't grant me the fifteen minutes for which I'd asked ... and the cops arrived, while I was still kicking.

SIX ...

I liked the guy. He was, without exception, the most humane cop I'd ever encountered ... and it wasn't a put-on. I didn't catch his name – not that that was too important – only his rank. Detective chief inspector. And, although he was throwing not only the book, but the whole damn library, into my teeth, he was doing it without animosity. Quietly. Unhurriedly. Like a grave-digger, who knows his job, reaches the required six-feet depth in no time at all, and without breaking into a sweat.

It was well past midnight, and I'd had a very heavy day. After the casino punch-up I'd been rattled around the forensic concrete-mixer a few times by a duo of detective sergeants whose muscles outweighed their brains; the usual thing – the bish-bash-bosh routine which some creeps fondly figure is the only way to detect crime – and, what with this and what Barlow had handed me, I looked slightly dented.

Then had come the D.C.I.

We didn't even use an interview room. We used his office; not a very flash office, but warm, and with a homely, 'lived in' atmosphere. The walls wouldn't have said 'No' to a lick of paint, and the carpet was a mite threadbare in places. The desk was stained and had a few cigarette burns around its edges. There was a cardboard box – one of those Weetabix empty cartons, you can pick up as makeshift packing-boxes, at any supermarket – alongside the desk. There was the usual mix of filing cabinets, shelves and book cases ... all the things a working office needs.

There was also a side-desk and, at the side-desk, sat a poker-faced, plainclothes man, with his notebook open, and his ballpoint at the ready.

The D.C.I. led me to a chair, near the desk, returned to the door, in order to close it, then did a return journey to the desk, to settle down for the big pow-wow.

He leaned back in the desk chair, linked his fingers across his stomach and grinned, as if at an old and valued friend.

'You've had a bashing, bonny lad,' he remarked, ruefully ... and the Geordie accent punched its way through the façade of Met language he'd been encouraged to use.

I nodded.

'Not all us, I hope,' he said.

'Some ... but not much.' My tongue played with a loosened tooth.

'No complaints, then?'

'Would it matter?'

'That depends.'

'On what?'

The grin came again, and he said, 'How loud you complained ... and who heard you.'

'You, for example?'

'If they've done *all* that ...'

'They haven't.'

'So-o ... how loud?'

'Little more than a whisper.'

'I can't hear whispers,' he said, then added, 'by the way ... smoke, if you feel like it. If you have any.'

'I haven't. Your blokes took them away from me.'

He patted his pockets, then tossed cigarettes and matches onto the desk top. I helped myself, and he waited until I was smoking before he spoke again.

He said, 'You've had the Official Caution? All the you're-not-obliged-to-say-anything patter?'

'Yeah.'

'You know what it means?'

'Yeah.'

'*Exactly* what it means? That it means what it says?'

'Yeah ... I know.'

'And the solicitor bit?'

'I've been told.'

'There's a phone there, on the desk.' He nodded. 'Any time you feel you need a solicitor, pick it up ... there'll be no argument.'

'I'm beyond a solicitor,' I said, bitterly.

'Aye.' He leaned forward, rested his forearms on the desk top, and said, 'I'll not kid you, bonny lad. You're in trouble.'

I inhaled cigarette smoke, then let the words, 'Don't I know it,' ride out on the exhalation.

He leaned sideways, dipped a hand into the Weetabix box, brought out a transparent plastic bag, and dropped it onto the table. The pendants, the rings, the stones ... despite the deadening effect of the plastic, they still sparkled life under the strip lighting.

'Twenty-five thousand,' he observed, gently.

'I'd have said slightly less.'

'That's Noble's valuation.'

'It's the valuation that counts,' I conceded.

'Did you have a buyer?' he asked.

'No.' I shook my head.

He smiled, and said, 'Would you tell me, if you had?'

'No,' I admitted. 'But it doesn't apply. I hadn't.'

'Just a lucky dip?' There was the faint tinge of scorn colouring the question.

'Not quite,' I said.

'Okay ... why Noble's?'

'Rawle put me onto it. Rawle's a...'

'We'll come to Rawle,' he interrupted, quietly. 'Eventually.'

'Sure.'

I didn't argue. I was well past arguing. Well past caring. Here was a man, prepared to treat me with a modicum of kindness – a modicum of dignity – so, he could take things at his own chosen speed and, whatever that speed happened to be, that was okay by me.

He touched the plastic bag, with a forefinger, and said, 'We found them in your car.'

'Yeah.'

'Your Volvo.'

'That's – that's where I left them,' I agreed.

'Parked in front of your house.'

'Eh?'

'In Putney.'

Some sort of surprised expression must have touched my face.

He said, 'Are you saying you parked it there? In front of your own place? With all this junk inside?'

'That's – that's where you found it,' I muttered.

'Come on, bonny lad,' he urged, gently. 'You can do better than that.'

'That's where you found it,' I repeated.

'Aye ... but where you *left* it?'

'If I say "Yes"?'

'Sorry, lad ... I won't believe you.'

'Yes.' I turned my head, looked at the plainclothes man, and said, 'Get it down, son. That's where I left the Volvo. Where you found it.'

The D.C.I. looked worried for a moment, then nodded, and said, 'It's what he wants ... get it down.'

Why?

That's the question. Why was I putting my head on the block? Why was I deliberately threading my arms into the sleeves of the strait-jacket? It's hard to explain ... but *I* knew. Call it an animal instinct for self-preservation.

The Volvo had been moved ... and, obviously, for a purpose. Equally obviously, by a certain party. Which, by logical progression, meant certain things.

Jones and his group – Dilton-Emmet and Willie Sagar, and God only knew who else – was out there, waiting. Listening. Ready. And, if I said the wrong thing...

Jesus!

I wanted to live. Whatever else, I wanted to live ... so I trimmed my answers to suit whatever *they* might have wanted.

The D.C.I. said, 'It's fair to tell you that I don't believe you.'

'No?'

He lighted a cigarette, then said, 'You're too good. You're a canny breaker, Martin.'

'Was ... once upon a time.'

'Still are. Noble's place proves that.'

I said, 'Things went wrong.'

He nodded slowly, and said, 'All right. We'll leave it at that.' He bent down to the Weetabix box, and produced the case of picklocks. 'These?' he asked, mildly, as he placed them alongside the plastic bag of loot.

'Mine,' I said.

'They're bonny.' He unzipped the case and stroked the picks and probes with the tips of his fingers. 'I've seen a few ... but none as good.'

There was no answer needed. I didn't waste time giving one.

He said, 'Would you – er – like to tell me where you got them?'

'The usual place.' I treated him to a weary smile. 'From a man in a pub. I forget which pub, I don't know the man's name ... and I couldn't *really* describe him.'

He stared into my eyes for a moment, then murmured, 'You wouldn't be getting awkward, bonny lad, would you?'

'I'm answering your questions,' I countered.

'I wouldn't call 'em "answers". Would you?'

'They're being recorded.'

'Aye. All the bull ... it's being recorded.'

'It's what I'll say in court.'

'The man-in-a-pub bullshit?'

'It's what I'll say.'

He shook his head, sadly, and murmured, 'They'll crucify you.'

'I know ... I'll still say it.'

He stared at me, for a moment, chewed his lip, then leaned back in his chair again, and linked his fingers across his middle.

The words, 'The experts don't love you any more, lad,' was prefixed with a quick, mischievous grin. 'The Chubb boys are going quietly crazy.'

'It's understandable.'

'For their peace of mind – for *my* peace of mind – how many other men could have pulled it? At a guess?'

I answered truthfully.

I said. 'None.' I nodded at the leather picklock case. '*I* couldn't, without those, and – for *your* peace of mind – that's the only set in existence ... and the man who made *them* is pushing up daisies.'

'The man in the pub?' he taunted, gently.

'Yeah ... the man in the pub.'

'Thank God for small mercies.' He gave an exaggerated sigh, then said, 'But, the alarm systems. Three of 'em. Foolproof ... that's what they each claim to be. You worked your way through all three.'

'I'm a clever man,' I said, immodestly.

'You're an unpopular man, lad.' He chuckled. 'So am I, come to that. I suggested that, when they'd worked out modifications, they let *you* loose on 'em ... just to be sure. They didn't like the idea.'

'Nevertheless, a good idea.' I smiled – a genuine smile –

for the first time since I couldn't remember when.

His next remark was a little off-putting ... it was so natural, and so friendly.

He said, 'D'you like cheese and pickle sandwiches?'

'Er – I – I ...'

'I do. And I'm feeling peckish.'

It wasn't some subtle catch, after all, so I nodded, and said, 'Yeah. I like cheese and pickle sandwiches.'

He turned to the plainclothes man, and said, 'Rustle 'em up, Ray. Three lots. And three beakers ... hot, strong and sweet. We'll give things a breather, while we eat.'

The plainclothes man said, 'Yes, sir,' closed his notebook and left the office.

SEVEN ...

It wasn't a come-on, either. I was waiting for it, but it didn't arrive. The now-there's-just-us-two-let's-talk-man-to-man garbage. He was above that; he was too decent an individual to be a liar, and too proud a man to try a con trick.

It really *was* a break in the questioning.

We settled back in our chairs and, when the tea and sandwiches arrived, we chatted about ordinary things. He was a Newcastle supporter – but of course – and the plainclothes man favoured Leeds United. My team was Derby, and we talked football. I swear ... *football*! We smoked cigarettes, we chewed sandwiches, we sipped tea, and we talked football.

You figure that's nothing? Nothing to get excited about? I tell you ...

I suddenly wanted to blub. To be so normal – to be so *ordinary* – after the last few days of being shark-bait. The contrast was damn near more than I could take, and I almost broke.

Then, the empty beakers and the empty plates were returned to the tray, the plainclothes man settled down at his side-desk, and the D.C.I. said, 'Back to business, bonny lad. Ray's taking it down ... and the telephone's still there.'

'Understood,' I choked. 'And – y'know ... thanks.'

EIGHT ...

From the Weetabix box came a knife and a wallet of seven-by-nine photographs. He placed the knife between us, on the desk top, then raised his eyes and looked at me.

He said, 'I mustn't put answers into your mouth, lad.'

'No.' I stared, fascinated, at the knife.

He said, 'We found it upstairs.'

'Upstairs?'

' "Small and Long. Property Valuers",' he said, dead-faced.

'Oh!'

'With the oxygen bottles, the hydrofluoric acid ... all the other gear you used.'

I said, 'Oh!' again, and continued to stare at the knife.

'Recognise it?' he asked.

'Yeah.' I nodded. 'But...'

'Careful,' he warned. 'There's a telephone there. My advice – for what it's worth ... use it.'

'I don't need a lawyer,' I breathed.

'It's your choice, bonny lad.'

'That's my knife,' I said, softly.

'It has your dabs on it.'

I swallowed, then said, 'I – I killed my wife with it ...'

'Easy!' He looked worried, then said, 'You've been cautioned, Martin. Nobody's twisting your arm. No promises. No inducements. No threats. You know exactly where you stand – exactly what you're saying ... right?'

'Right.' I nodded.

'And, you've had my advice.'

'I've had your advice,' I agreed, 'and, I'm telling you that I used *that* knife on my wife. I stabbed her to death with it ... *but I didn't take the knife up into that office.*'

Instead of answering, he pushed the wallet of photographs across the top of the desk, towards me.

I picked them up and examined them, one at a time.

About a dozen. I didn't count them ... but, about a dozen. Police photographs. Black and white; shiny, stark and without pose or art perspective. The upper office, next to Noble's shop. The equipment I'd left there. The battered furniture. And *she* was there, on the floor. On her back, alongside the desk. Her eyes were still open. The slash marks showed black, and vivid. Dead ... so very obviously dead. *There* ... in that upper room ... where I'd left the gear ... where she *hadn't* been ... where...

'Comment?' asked the D.C.I., gently.

I steeled myself from going completely crazy, and said, 'It's her.'

'Your wife?'

'Yeah. My wife ... Muriel.'

'And?'

'I killed her.' I glanced at the knife, on the desk top. 'That's what I killed her with.'

'Why?'

'Barlow,' I breathed.

'Barlow?'

I said, 'This evening – when your blokes dragged me away from him ... I was killing *him*.'

'Oh!'

'She – er – she was going to leave me. For him.'

He looked unhappy, then said, 'Jealousy. It's the...'

'Not jealousy,' I interrupted.

'You said...'

'Possession.'

'Oh!'

'There's a difference.' My voice was hoarse with emotion. 'I'd given her everything. I'd gone straight, for her sake. No other women ... nothing like that. I'd given her every damn thing she'd asked for. Maybe – maybe I'm incapable of what you call "love" – I wouldn't know – but I'm capable of generosity ... and she was given a hell of a lot of that. I demanded something in return. Loyalty.'

'And now?'

The man was unique. He could crawl into my brain, seek, then ask, the one question I didn't want him to ask; and, moreover, ask it in a tone of voice which demanded an answer.

I answered him, and I spoke the truth.

'I wish I hadn't,' I said, flatly.

He nodded, as if satisfied, and said, 'You know what love is, bonny lad ... now.'

He lighted a new cigarette, tossed the packet and matches across the desk, and I joined him in the fag stakes, before the interview continued.

He said, 'She wasn't killed where we found her.'

'No. At home. In the kitchen.'

'She'd been dead a few days.'

'Yeah.'

'She'd ...' He hesitated, as if seeking words, then said, 'The pathologist mentioned refrigeration ... something about refrigeration.'

'A deep freeze.'

'Y'mean you...'

'Not me. Rawle.'

'Oh!'

'Rawle shifted the body. I asked him. He shifted it. I thought he'd buried it, somewhere. He hadn't. He'd put it in cold storage ... as personal insurance.'

'I see.' He dipped into the Weetabix carton again, then placed a Luger automatic on the surface of the desk. He said, 'So-o ... this?'

I'd seen that Luger before. I was damn sure. The last time I'd seen it, it had been nudging my gut and the guy holding it was sporting a full set of red whiskers. It was the same gun ... as surely as morning follows night.

The D.C.I. said, 'That's the gun that killed Rawle and his man. The ballistics boys don't make mistakes.'

'Yeah ... I know.'

'And a man out Burnt Oak way. An electrician. A man called...'

'Called Len.' I ended the sentence for him.

'And the gun was found in your car. No prints ... but found in your car.'

'But, that's...' I stopped in mid-sentence.

'Yes?' The D.C.I. waited, patiently.

'There – there *was* a gun in the car, but...'

'Yes?' repeated the D.C.I., after another silence.

'It – it doesn't matter, really ... does it?' I muttered, wearily. 'I mean – y'know ... it doesn't really *matter*. You can prove it. That's all that counts ... isn't it?'

'Strong circumstantial evidence,' said the D.C.I., quietly. 'Which is ... *proof*.'

'You want the honest answer, lad?'

I nodded.

He said, 'Aye. It's only my opinion, of course. I'm not God ... I could be wrong. I think we've enough proof. We've had convictions on less ... a lot less.'

NINE...

For a moment, I stopped listening. For a moment I wasn't there – wasn't in that homely office of that very human detective chief inspector – but, instead, I was in a very crummy, upper office in Newman Street.

Listening to another voice. A cold, expressionless voice.

A voice without emotion. A voice devoid of all mercy.

The voice was saying...

'Whichever way you turn, you're in the net ... Whichever way you turn, you're in the net ... Whichever way you turn, you're in the net ... Whichever way you turn...'

And, I knew.

I was the patsy ... but good!

Rawle had talked, before they'd shot him. He'd told them everything and, from that moment, it had been easy.

Who the hell was going to believe the Athens thing? Who the hell was going to *believe?*

TEN...

I'd dropped my chin onto my chest, and was mumbling, 'I'm in the net. God Almighty! I'm *really* in the bloody net.'

'What?' The D.C.I. stopped saying whatever it was he was saying, frowned non-understanding, and said, 'What net?'

I pinched the bridge of my nose, rubbed a palm across my aching eyes, and said, 'You wouldn't believe me, if I told you.'

'Try me.'

'No.' I gave him a bone-weary smile. Maybe he thought I was tired – physically tired – but he was wrong. The smile was a capitulation. An unconditional surrender to what I knew damn well I couldn't lick. I said, 'Ask your questions. I'll answer 'em.'

'Look – there's nobody...'

'I know. Nobody's twisting my arm. At least, *you're* not.'

'Okay, bonny lad.' He touched the Luger. 'What about this?'

'What about it?'

'We like to know where you get these things.'

I almost laughed, as I said, 'The same man. The same pub.'

He sighed, resignedly.

'Get it down, I'll sign it,' I promised.

He shrugged, and said, 'It shot Rawle.'

'Yeah.'

'It shot Rawle's minder.'

'Yeah ... I know that, too.'

'It was found in your car.'

'I believe you.'

'You had reason to hate Rawle.'

'He shoved my wife into an ice-box ... I had reason to hate him.'

'Motive?' he suggested, gently.

I said, 'It's a strong enough motive.'

'And the minder?' he asked.

I said, 'Anybody who wanted to shoot Rawle had to blast a way through the minder first ... okay?'

He nodded, slowly, then said, 'That's three murders you've admitted, Martin. It's only fair to remind you.'

'Thanks.' I gave him a very watery smile, and added, 'Four ... counting Anne.'

'Your daughter?'

'Don't tell me you don't know.'

'Aye ... we know.'

'I strangled her, too.'

'Why?'

I took a deep breath, then said, 'The lousiest motive of all. Temper. We had an argument ... I even forget what it was all about. I grabbed her, and squeezed. That's all.'

'Diminished responsibility?' he suggested, gently.

'Don't make me laugh.'

'It's a plea.'

'A hell of a lot of good *that's* going to do. Three cold-blooded – one hot-blooded ... that's *real* nit-picking.'

'I make it *four* cold-blooded,' he said, solemnly.

'Oh! You mean the Burnt Oak killing? Len?'

He nodded.

In a very stonewall voice, I said, 'Yeah – the same gun ... but, for the moment, I forget the motive.'

He dipped his hand into the Weetabix box and, this time, it came out with a shoe box filled with notes.

'Money,' he said. 'Your dabs are on the box. The box was found in your car. The boffins have linked the box with a shelf in the workroom. Wire fibres. Flux. Dust. They can put the box on the shelf. We can put your fingers on the box. Five thousand ... that's motive enough, wouldn't you say?'

'Motive enough,' I agreed, slowly. 'Five thousand smackers is one hell of a motive to talk your way out of.'

'But, you'll try?'

'No.' I shook my head. 'I won't even try.'

'Er...' He rubbed the side of his nose with a forefinger, then said, 'Your wife – your dead wife ... why take her up into that office?'

'What do you do with a corpse?' I countered. 'She had to go somewhere.'

'From the – er – refrigerator?'

'Yeah.'

'By the way, where was the refrigerator?'

'I forget.'

He smiled his friendly smile, and said, 'Come on, bonny lad. You've told the truth, so far. Don't start being daft at this point.'

'That's it, friend.' I put flat finality into my voice. 'You have enough – you've more than enough ... you don't need more. As of this moment, I don't know. I forget. And, I'm never going to remember. What I've told you – make it into a statement ... I'll sign.'

'You don't have to. There's nobody...'

'I'll sign,' I interrupted. 'I won't retract. Not a word. You don't even have to put "I'm sorry" at the end of it ... because that wouldn't help.'

'No ... not much,' he agreed, sadly.

ELEVEN ...

They stood me in the dock, next morning; an application for committal to custody, pending enquiries. They read out the charges; five murders, the theft of the jewellery, G.B.H. against Barlow plus odds and ends about guns, and things, just to block up all the bolt-holes.

The magistrate listened, then asked me the usual bull – whether I wished to say anything – then got the shock of his middle-aged life, when I said, 'Yes.'

He eyed me sternly, and said, 'I must warn you, Martin. You're under no obligation to say anything, at this stage.'

'Yeah ... I know that.'

'I see you're not represented. You haven't sought advice from a solicitor. I think...'

'I'm not going to need a solicitor. Or a barrister.'

He looked shocked, then said, 'You mean you intend to conduct your own defence? If so, I feel I must warn you...'

'No defence.'

'Oh!'

'Just something I want to say. That's all.'

He leaned forward and held a short, whispered conversation with the clerk of the court, then straightened, looked across at me, and said, 'This is a court of record, Martin. You know what that means, do you?'

'I know what it means.'

'It means that any statement you elect to make will be carefully noted. Verbatim, in fact. And that statement will be read out at whichever higher court eventually hears your case.'

'I know what I'm doing,' I said.

'In that case...' The magistrate spread his palms in token of surrender. 'Say what you have to say.'

I cleared my throat, and steadied my voice, before I spoke.

Then, I said, 'All my life I've been what society is pleased to call "a criminal". Part of my life I've held my criminality in abeyance ... but it's always been there, as a part of my mental make-up. Until recently I was always what I like to call a "clean" criminal. I stole property ... the record of my previous convictions tells its own tale. What violence I had, I kept in check. I have now committed murder ... I realise that these words are the equivalent to a plea of "Guilty", and that is the plea I intend to make.

'But – forgive me, if I appear to pontificate – there is a degree of criminality which is lower, even, than that required to commit murder. It concerns theft. A peculiar theft. The theft of a man's mind. The theft of a man's soul. Few creatures on God's earth are capable of that degree of evil. Few men possess that degree of amorality. But, those who do are vermin – they are the rats of the human race – and, recently, I have had contact with them. I doubt if I will ever again be clean. But, this I know ... I plead "Guilty" to multiple murder, and every other crime with which I am charged, knowing that, even so, my misdeeds are *nothing*, when placed alongside theirs.' I nodded, as a token bow of thanks to the magistrate, for granting me the right to say what I wished to say, then added, 'Thank you, sir, for hearing me out. What I've just said isn't a plea. It isn't an excuse, or an explanation. I wish it to be placed on record ... no more. To be recorded, in order to ensure that it is never forgotten.'

The magistrate motioned to the two uniformed constables, and the constables turned me, in the dock, to descend the steps leading down into the cells.

For the first time, I glanced at the men and women in the public gallery.

Willie Sagar was in the second row. Our eyes met, and a quick smile touched his lips, and his head moved in a barely perceptible shake ... then he was hidden by the surround of the dock, as I moved down the steps.

And, I knew!

My fine little speech. It was going to be killed. It was already dead! ... as dead as every other thing those bastards wished to destroy.

TWELVE..

Its distribution by involuntary human agency may indeed be compared with that of the cockroach, which man has likewise carried with him over the globe.

RAT

The Harmsworth Encyclopaedia